Penguin Crime Fiction
Filmi, Filmi, Inspector Ghote

H. R. F. Keating was born at St Leonards-on-Sea, Sussex, in 1926 and went to school at Merchant Taylors. After a period of what he describes as 'totally undistinguished service' in the army, which he joined the day the war ended, he went to Trinity College, Dublin, where he became a Scholar in modern literature. From Dublin he went to Wiltshire as a journalist and, before he began devoting his time to writing, he had worked in Fleet Street on the *Daily Telegraph* and *The Times*.

His first crime novel, *Death and the Visiting Firemen*, came out in 1959 and *The Perfect Murder* won the Crime Writers' Association Golden Dagger for 1964. He was Chairman of the Crime Writers' Association 1970 to 1971, is crime fiction reviewer for *The Times* and has published a study of detective stories of the 1930s, *Murder Must Appetize*. Other books by H. R. F. Keating are *Inspector Ghote Plays a Joker*, *Inspector Ghote Breaks an Egg*, *Inspector Ghote Goes by Train*, *Inspector Ghote Trusts the Heart*, *The Underside*, *Bats Fly Up for Inspector Ghote* and *A Long Walk to Wimbledon*. In 1977 he edited *Agatha Christie: First Lady of Crime*.

The author is married to Sheila Mitchell, the actress, and has three sons and a daughter.

H. R. F. Keating

Filmi, Filmi, Inspector Ghote

Penguin Books

Penguin Books Ltd, Harmondsworth,
Middlesex, England
Penguin Books, 625 Madison Avenue,
New York, New York 10022, U.S.A.
Penguin Books Australia Ltd, Ringwood,
Victoria, Australia
Penguin Books Canada Ltd, 2801 John Street,
Markham, Ontario, Canada L3R 1B4
Penguin Books (N.Z.) Ltd, 182–190 Wairau Road,
Auckland 10, New Zealand

First published by William Collins Sons & Company Ltd
in their Collins Crime Club Series 1976
Published in Penguin Books 1979

Made and printed in Great Britain by
Cox & Wyman Ltd,
London, Reading and Fakenham
Set in Intertype Times

Author's Note

I have taken the little liberty of listing once as
a set of marginally disreputable characters the
names of a number of Indian writers in English.
They are used only by way of recording, if in a
somewhat paradoxical way, my gratitude for
the help I have had from them, mostly through
their writing – much of which is unjustly unknown
in other English-speaking countries – occasionally
more directly.

Chapter 1

The Deputy Commissioner was reading a *filmi* magazine. There was no mistaking it. Inspector Ghote had come hurrying into his big airy office in response to a crisp summons on the intercom and he had caught him in the act. The head of the Bombay Police Crime Branch leaning back in his chair reading a trashy magazine devoted to huge pictures of film stars and the gossip of the *filmi duniya.*

Ghote stood there stiff with dismay.

If only he had had the sense to have taken one quick glance through the little square of glass in the door. But no. It had been a long while since he had received orders direct from the Deputy Commissioner and the thought of what he might hear had swamped everything else in his mind. A big case perhaps, influential people involved, a chance to put himself in good standing with the senior-most officers. And now he had caught the Deputy Commisioner out.

What should he do?

He decided on a small cough. And as soon as the sound – it had unfortunately come out rather more like the strangulated bellow of an affronted bullock – had broken the quiet of the room he swung round and pretended to be occupied in closing the door with proper care.

'Ah, Ghote. Yes. Come in, man.'

He turned and walked smartly towards the enormous desk with its telephones and its neatly arranged files, its big blotter and its presentation pens. And the *filmi* magazine was still open in the Deputy Commissioner's hands, the star's face on its cover plain to see – it was the famous cutting profile of Ravi Kumar, the No. 1 Superstar of them all – as well as the advertisement on the back for Somebody-or-Other's Suiting.

Ghote placed himself at attention behind the four chairs drawn up in front of the big desk.

'Yes, sir?' he said.

The Deputy Commissioner laid down the magazine, sat forward and regarded him steadily through liquidly intelligent eyes.

'Ghote,' he said, 'I have a priority case for you. Just been notified. Emergency call from Talkiestan Studios.'

For a moment he paused, as if the news was almost too big to break.

'Dhartiraj has been killed,' he said.

'Dhartiraj? The star?'

Ghote, whose knowledge of the film world hardly extended beyond an adolescent admiration for the top stars of that day, was not altogether sure what kind of an actor Dhartiraj was. He even just wondered whether after all he was not a well-known wrestler.

But no, he had been killed at the famous Talkiestan Studios, one of the all-India known names in the great Bombay film industry. He must be a star. Killed in suspicious circumstances plainly, and he, Inspector Ghote, put in charge of the investigation.

Suddenly his heart beneath his open-necked checked shirt began to thud in awed delight.

But, as quickly, other thoughts rose up. Incredulous, doubt-tinged thoughts.

'But, sir,' he said. 'Sir, is it me only that you are putting in charge?'

Then, feeling abruptly that he should not have voiced any fears about his own ability to tackle any case, however influential the victim, he hastily found a reason for his words.

'Sir, I am not at all knowing the *filmi duniya*, sir. I am not at all a film world person.'

'I should think not,' the Deputy Commissioner said with a trace of tartness. 'I would not expect any of my officers to bother their heads with this sort of thing.'

And he jabbed his finger straight down on to the sharply handsome face of Ravi Kumar.

8

'Had to send out for this myself,' he added. 'Just to get my bearings, find out that Dhartiraj was a great player of Villains and so forth.'

'Yes, sir,' said Ghote, as if he had never for a moment wondered why his chief should have been going through such frivolous reading matter.

'Yes,' the Deputy Commissioner went on with a faint sigh, 'I suppose I shall have to let it be known I am taking a personal interest in the case. But—'

His eyes came up and he looked Ghote inflexibly in the face.

'But I want it clearly understood, Inspector, that it is you and you alone who are investigating the affair. If it comes to the Courts eventually, it will be you and you alone who would be chief prosecution witness.'

And again from Ghote's heart rich thuds of pride and pleasure began to beat out. But this time he did nothing to silence them.

'So it is definitely a question of murder, sir?' he asked, putting into his voice all the seriousness and purpose he could command.

'Yes, Ghote, it is a question of murder.'

When Ghote approached the Talkiestan Studios, his head still full of the Deputy Commissioner's promises of technical backing and with the sight of him sitting, as he himself had clicked heels and left, looking at his telephones almost as if one of them had particularly told him whom to select to take charge, he found the studio gates besieged.

Plainly the news of Dhartiraj's death had begun to leak out. Through his car windscreen, only the tops of the tall iron gates, with the legend 'Talkiestan Studios' in huge white letters above them, could be seen for the backs of dozens of eager Bombayites intent on pushing, scrambling, edging or even crawling their way to a view of the Studios' compound. Ragged shirts and laundered ones, bare backs and sari-clad ones, flowing kurtas of purest undyed white *khaddi* and workday uniforms of messengers, postmen and peons in all shades of green and khaki jostled and elbowed and struggled for place.

'Horn through,' Ghote snapped out to his driver. 'Push on, push on.'

On the far side of those gates, which he saw now were being defended by a couple of harassed-looking Gurkha chowkidars and a tall fancifully turbaned Pathan, lay his case. There somewhere would be the body of the dead star. There the witnesses. The suspects. Even perhaps the murderer.

'Horn through, man, horn through.'

With savage little klaxon blasts reinforced by shouts, fierce and commanding as they could make them, through each of the open windows, inch by inch they crept their way forward. Then, when at last the heavy bumper of the car was in actual contact with the rusty iron of the gates, Ghote leaned yet further out, selected the chowkidar who looked most in control and barked at him the two words 'Police. Open.'

The man, one of the two short-statured stubby-faced Gurkhas, gathered his two partners and then with a key painfully extracted from his pocket undid the heavy padlock keeping the gate chain tight. At once the pressure of the crowd outside began to force back the two tall gates. The chowkidars pushed against them with straining backs. Ghote's driver, needing no instructions, eased the car forward so that it never ceased to block the slowly increasing gap. The moment the gates were wide enough the chowkidars redoubled their efforts and held them steady. The car scraped its way through.

Inside the compound it was clear that the tragedy had brought all normal activity to a halt. People of every sort were running excitedly here, there and everywhere in search of some new titbit of rumour. Small groups came momentarily together, their voices rising to a wild clacking, only suddenly to break up again. Others shouted across to friends the cream of what they knew. Yet others yelled orders for quiet. Ghote, leaving his driver to help the chowkidars at the gates, stood looking on at them all, determined quickly as he could to get his bearings.

Extras. Some of these people would be film extras. He felt a quick rose tinge of pride at working that out, the unexpected readiness with which the word had come into his mind. Yes, definitely those at first unplaceable men and women, looking like idlers who should not have been inside the compound at all, would be film extras. And that huddle of women under the big gul mohar tree, somewhat better dressed, though their saris were flashily bold, they would be extras of a better class or small-part actresses. Yes.

And others in the spate-eddying crowd were easier to account for. The clerks, the smartly dressed stenos, the peons and messengers. Studios would need those as well as any other business. And coolies, even if in this strange world it was not easy to say exactly what their tasks would be. But simple enough to pick them out in their loincloths or tattered shorts as the necessary labour to move whatever had to be moved in the business of film-making, to haul things up and lower them down. There were a fair number of Ghati women about too, dark-skinned creatures from the hills with their coarse-coloured saris drawn tightly over their hips, even less skilled labour for even simpler unknown tasks. A sudden waft of the smell of new-sawn wood told him that a trio of excited gossipers beside a grotesque shape of papier-mâché moulding, once bright, now washed out from lying too long in the sun, were carpenters. A film studio would need plenty of carpenters.

Yes, and there, those two men in heavily embroidered kurtas, standing nose to nose and talking with deep resonant voices and wide gestures, they must be proper actors. Proper film actors.

For a moment he felt a sinking. Those would be the sort of witnesses he would be having to deal with. And they were not the sort he understood.

But he would deal with them. Just let them try any of their tricks. When it came down to it, people were people, whatever their high and flighty claims. And people could be made to tell the truth, or be caught out in their lies. They could have their wild talk and their prideful over-claims held down, if there was someone determined to do it.

He swung round and went back to the tall Pathan chowkidar, standing puffing beside the re-closed gates.

'Who is in charge here?'

'In charge, Inspector sahib? There are many *burra sahibs* in Studios.'

'I want whoever can tell me what happened to Dhartiraj. *Ek dum!*'

'Oh my God, yes. Yes, Inspector sahib. I am thinking it is Production Manager sahib you are wanting.'

'Then take me to him, *jaldi, jaldi.*'

He followed the tall, loping Pathan through the turbulence. The whole compound was a jumble of different single-storey buildings, mostly wooden-built with deep verandas in front, almost as confusing at first encounter as the excited crowds milling this way and that wherever they went.

'Dance rehearsal room, sahib,' his guide said suddenly, as they passed a tall construction in dirty white slabbing. 'Air-condition. Very good.'

'Yes,' Ghote said.

He spotted among the jabbering clerks and extras and coolies a man carrying a curious plastic tray in front of him, as if he was some sort of vendor, and an unaccountable recollection of something he believed he did not know told him that the fellow was a make-up man. He felt a new spurt of confidence.

Perhaps he was not as incapable of dealing with the *filmi duniya* as he had told the Deputy Commissioner.

Here and there, as they made their way through the crowd and past the confusion of buildings, cars were parked, mostly familiar and dusty Ambassadors or Fiats. But one or two, in the shade under trees, were magnificent and foreign. Stars' vehicles, he said to himself. Yes.

Posters on the trees, fixed high up and protected with transparent plastic, with the names of films that stirred faint memories in his mind, shone down at him with the words across them in huge letters 'Silver Jubilee'. Yes, films that had run in their original cinema for an uninterrupted twenty-five weeks. And there, a title he doubly recognized because he had taken his Protima and little Ved to see it, was one with the coveted words 'Golden Jubilee' plastered across. Fifty weeks of continuous showing.

So that had come from these very studios.

He felt obscurely that he had taken another firm step into the mysterious world ahead of him. Yes, he might have to make guesses from time to time and there would be things he did not at first understand, but he would be a match for it all. He would be. He must be.

Two or three chickens fled squawking from under the Pathan's heavy sandals. Above, the crows, infected by the human agitation below, cawed and croaked even more noisily than usual. And, as they approached a low brick-built structure, a degree more impressive than the other offices they had passed, a new note was added to the encircling din, the shrilling of many telephones.

The news of the calamity must be getting out. Reporters by the score would be checking on the rumour. Before many minutes, indeed, they would be swarming down on to the Studios, bribing their way in, asking questions, taking pictures. He would have to be pretty damn sharp with them. See that they kept well out of the way.

The tall Pathan led him up on to the veranda of the brick-built building and flung open one of the cabin doors.

'Production Manager sahib,' he said loudly, 'it is the CID Inspector.'

The Production Manager, a grizzled stumpy man wearing a bright orange shirt with Bombay scenes printed on it, the Taj Hotel with its tall crowned Intercontinental tower, poor old chopped-down Flora Fountain, the dazzling upspringing sky-scraper of the Overseas Communications Building, was attempting to answer two telephones simultaneously. To Ghote's quick gratification, he slammed them both down at once.

'CID,' he said. 'Thank God, you have come.'

Ghote drew back his shoulders.

'All hell is being let loose here,' the Production Manager went on. 'We are badly, badly needing police co-operation.'

'But there are men from the local station here already, isn't it?' Ghote said.

'Oh yes, yes. But such fellows are no good at all. What we are wanting is some tough CID to clear out all these extras and riffraffs so we can deal with the mess to the best of our ability.'

'The CID does not carry out crowd control,' Ghote said with sharpness. 'I am here to investigate the death of Mr Dhartiraj.'

'Yes, yes. You can see Studio Publicity Manager and fix up with him what story is to be put out. With all these damned phones ring-ringing all the time the sooner we have agreed statement the better.'

'Listen to me,' Ghote shouted with sudden ferocity. 'I am not here to help with studio publicity. I am here to carry out investigation. Were you yourself on the scene when the tragic occurrence took place?'

'No. No.'

The Production Manager was startled into silence. Ghote jumped quickly into the pause he had created.

'Well then,' he said, 'who was at the scene? That is the fellow I am wanting to see.'

'But – But that would be Director Ghosh. Bhabani Ghosh, twelve jubilees in five years. He is the one who is directing *Khoon Ka Gaddi*.'

'*Khoon Ka Gaddi*?' Ghote asked.

It must be the title of the film they were making. But the Production Manager had spoken the words with such awe, as if they were bound to be rich with meaning for whoever heard them, that he felt abruptly lost again. *Khoon Ka Gaddi*. It meant *Cushion of Blood*. No, surely not. Ah, yes, *gaddi* in the sense of a rajah's seat of honour. A throne. Yes, *Throne of Blood*, that sounded more likely.

'Yes, yes,' said the Production Manager, rapidly regaining his former bounce in face of this ignorance. 'The mightiest historical ever made. *Khoon Ka Gaddi*, screenplay by Dr Arvind Bhatt, Litt.D., from *Macbeth* which is by William Shakespeare.'

'I know *Macbeth*,' Ghote stated sharply.

He was not going to let this fellow walk over him. And, besides, it was almost true. The play had been one of his set books for Inter, until the syllabus had been unexpectedly changed. And, as he had always liked to be well in advance with his work, he had read most of it. Well, Acts One and Two certainly, and perhaps more.

'Yes,' he repeated. 'Well I am knowing *Macbeth*. But where is Mr Bhabani Ghosh? If he was the principal witness, then it is him I am wanting to see.'

'But he is there,' the Production Manager answered. 'There. At the scene of the crime.'

'The scene of the crime? Then take me to him straightaway. Take yourself, if you please. I have no time for hanging about.'

The scene of the crime. That was where he ought to be. There. Where it had happened. Seeing for himself. Investigating. Taking charge. Taking the case by the scruff of the neck, by God. At the scene of the crime.

Chapter 2

Marching out behind the once more subdued Production Manager, Ghote felt a pulsing of pleasure at the speed with which that stumpy orange-shirted figure was trotting down the veranda steps. To talk about the Studios' publicity, what self-centred madness. A murder had been committed. And its perpetrator had to be found. What was needed was —

'Production Manager sahib.'

The bellow through a jerked open window behind them was so loud that, though it was not his name that had been shouted, he came to a total halt on the top veranda step. The Production Manager froze as if he had been struck solid by the hand of God himself.

When, after a second of statue stillness, he turned cowedly round Ghote saw that his face bore an expression of such abjectness that it really seemed as if he was indeed confronting a god of old made flesh once more. His lips chewed hard at nothing as he endeavoured to get out a single word.

'Sethji?' he pronounced at last. 'You called, Sethji?'

Ghote followed the direction of his cringing stare, wondering at the effect that the Seth of the Studios, the Producer, the man of money and power could have. It was certainly very different from the way things went in his own world. There, if the Commissioner himself should address him he would certainly come to attention and answer with plentiful 'sirs'. But he would not touch any feet. And that, in all but actual fact, was what was happening here.

At the jerked-open window the god himself looked out, his name painted in large letters of gold under a plastic panel on the door just beside him, 'Mr Chagan Lal'. Seth Chagan Lal. A face of hard and solid fat with two small unyielding eyes and the straight slit of a little closed-up mouth. Above, a hard black boat-shaped cap, and below, the top of a pudgy body in a coat of white silk ornamented with pure gold buttons, pushed to popping point by the hard pressure of the flesh beneath.

'Production Manager sahib, you are taking away the CID wallah they have sent.'

It was an accusation.

The Production Manager looked suddenly, inside that orange shirt with its bold black designs, like a too small shop-window dummy.

'Sethji.' A small sound emerged from him. 'Sethji, I – I did not know. It was . . .'

'If they are sending to investigate the murder of one of my stars, I am wanting to see, isn't it?'

The voice came in sharp successive small bursts of thunder.

'Sethji, he is here.'

The Production Manager pushed a chopped-down gesture towards Ghote. It said, in so far as it dared, that he should go in at once and talk to the Seth.

Ghote debated in himself whether he should decline. He was after all not someone to be summoned. He was in his own person the chosen representative of the law, here to investigate the death of a nation's idol, a star.

At the open window Seth Chagan Lal remained unmoving.

Perhaps, as in any case sooner or later he would have to be interviewed, perhaps this was as good a time as any.

He crossed the broad veranda and opened the door with the Seth's name on it.

The office in which he found himself, stepping at once into an air-conditioned coolness that was instant luxury to the skin, was enormous, far larger than the Deputy Commissioner's back at Headquarters, larger than that of the Commissioner himself. All along the wall at the back ran a deep sofa, evidently the place where the outer-most circle of the Seth's suppliants sat when at last they were admitted to the great man's presence. It was covered in a flower-patterned material. A large area of dark red wall-to-wall carpeting had to be crossed next before coming to a small array of chairs, very modern-looking in black leather and gleaming chromium tubing. And between these and the great man's desk there was another five or six feet of uncrossable red carpet.

But what a desk it was. In a wild comparison that abruptly invaded his head, Ghote reckoned that it was only a little smaller in area than the whole of the bedroom in his own home. Its top was a single sheet of heavy glass, supported some six inches above the great dark and gleaming wood of the structure itself. Under it could be seen posters for films that must have achieved some special honour. On top of the glass there was, on the right, a magnificent table-lamp crowned by a shade of heavy red silk with beside it, like a fleet of small ships at anchor underneath a huge lighthouse, a dozen thick pens and pencils in dull and solid gold. To the left, there were seven telephones.

On the wall behind there could be seen the golden grille of the immense air-conditioner and the battered green-painted door of a very large safe.

Seth Chagan Lal waddled stiffly round to the huge chair behind the desk and sat down. Only then did Ghote take in that at one corner of the enormous piece of furniture there was sitting, perched on a very small stool-like chair, a very small secretary, an Anglo-Indian girl to judge by the skirt and blouse she wore and the lengths of shapely, but small, legs dangling down.

The Seth thrust a mess of papers and documents in a green leather folder towards her.

'Take,' he said. 'Write some nice answers. And ring them also at Cotton Exchange. Say to cover New York without fail.'

The diminutive girl took the folder, contrived in one rapid movement to reduce to order its this-way-and-that confusion, tucked it under her arm and minced past Ghote to the door, leaving behind a momentary fragrance of flowery talcum powder.

'Sit,' said the Seth, giving Ghote a single sharp look.

Ghote marched across to the chair nearest the great desk and lowered himself stiffly on to its very edge, though he was unable not to acknowledge the padded give of the leather beneath him.

'Mr Lal,' he said firmly. 'My name is Ghote, Inspector Ghote of Crime Branch CID, and I have been put in charge – '

'*Khoon Ka Gaddi* must go on. That is the first thing to be said.'

The Seth's little eyes in their hard encasing of fat bored straight into him.

'I realize, Mr – '

'In India there are two crores of people buying cinema seat each day. Twenty million sums of, let us say, rupees three each. I am not going to let the distributors think that my film will not take its share of them.'

The glare from the fat-encased eyes did not slacken by so much as a pin's width.

'Did you know that there are four hundred–five hundred films made here each year? Every one of them set to take money from mine. That is why *Khoon Ka Gaddi* must not stop.'

'Yes, Mr Lal, I well realize that – '

'It is not arty-warty films I am making. It is not Best Direction I am worrying about next week when it is Filmfare Awards. No, I am well knowing what it is that people are wanting, and that I am giving.'

Abruptly he inclined forward across the huge glass expanse of the desk top, cutting short Ghote's intervention even as it came to his lips. A look that might have been a smile fixed itself on his face.

'I was a poor boy once,' he said. 'Poor. Poor. And to my native place near Hyderabad there came one day a touring talkie. Then it was that I saw what a different world it could bring. And that is what is wanted in film line. That. A different world. With jewels. With far, far places. With music. With some really sexy scenes. And that is what still today I tell my directors to give.'

'Yes, yes. And I understand that the death of –'

'When I was beginning I did not have the money even to buy one story. Just enough for a song only. But I bought what I knew was good, what I knew the people would like, would sing, sing, sing themselves. And I persuaded a star, a big star then, to sign, though I had almost to drag him there for the *mahurat* shot so that I could say the film had been blessed and had begun. But when I played over that song to the distributors I began to get my money. Little by little. Three years it took to make that film. Three years, and then house-fulls all the first ten weeks. A real box-office grosser from the start.'

Ghote decided it must not go on any longer. He jumped to his feet and leant in his turn across the great glass expanse.

'Mr Lal. I am the Investigating Officer in the case of Mr Dhartiraj deceased. Deceased upon your premises. Sir, it is because that death took place on these premises that I decided to hear any statement you had to make first. But I am not going to be delayed from visiting the scene of the crime.'

'The scene of the crime?'

The Seth's fat-hard face had darkened.

But at least, Ghote thought, he listened to what I said.

'Inspector, this is the scene of the crime. This.'

And the Seth's clenched little fist came down so hard on the big sheet of glass that it gave out a deep booming note and even bent a little under the impact.

'Inspector, today it is very different matter with a Fifteen Arts production. Today I am not having to go round with one song only to the distributors. Today I can demand and get twenty-five lakhs of rupees per film per territory. Inspector, for *Khoon Ka Gaddi* it will be more. That film is a very-very big investment. And with Dhartiraj dead and eight reels in the cans only the situation is very-very serious.'

'Yes, Mr Lal, but – '

'Inspector, I am not wanting any scandals. That is the point, Inspector. Very well, very well, we shall have quickly-quickly to find a new star. And, very well, new shooting there will have to be, though that must be kept to a minimum-minimum. But nothing else is to go wrong. *Khoon Ka Gaddi* is going to be finished on schedule. And it is going to be an all-time hit film when it is finished. Touts at every cinema will be asking more-more for tickets than has ever before been demanded. Do you understand that?'

Ghote sat back in his chair again carefully. He had felt the Seth's sheer will flinging itself against him like a wild but deeply powerful monsoon sea. And he knew that he must not let it overwhelm him.

'Sir,' he said slowly. 'I am having to make one thing clear. A murder has taken place, and in due course there will be a person to be charged under Section 201 of the Indian Penal Code. Sir, if that person comes to hand – and I will be sparing of no effort to achieve that eventuality – then that charge will be made, whatever effect it may or may not have upon the progress of your film or upon Fifteen Arts Films Private Limited.'

For long seconds Seth Chagan Lal sat perfectly still. His blubber-hard face betrayed not a jot of surprise at his having been addressed in such terms. The little eyes expressed no flare of resentment.

'Very good, Inspector,' he said at last, 'you have had your say. I do not know whether you had thought before you have spoken, thought that a person of my interests would have also influence. But you have spoken.'

He put out a pudgy hand and minutely straightened one of the thick gold pens that lay beside the tall tablelamp.

'And now,' he went on, his voice still at the same low pitch, 'now I will have my say. Inspector, I am a man who gets his way. It is not without hurting people that I have risen up from a poor clerk first coming to Bombay to where I am today. And I still have a long way to go, Inspector. A long-long way. And nothing and no one is going to stop me.'

He leant back a little bit.

'Inspector, it would be best if you were not one of the people who stood in my path.'

Abruptly he reached under the glass of the desk top and pressed a bell-push that sounded a discreet buzz somewhere behind Ghote. At once the little Anglo-Indian secretary came in, carrying her shorthand notebook.

Ghote got up and made his way out past her. He did not feel it was necessary to say good-bye to the Seth.

But, as he stepped from the luxurious coolness of the big office into the dry and dusty sunlight, his mind was hammeringly at work.

He had had a warning. That much was more than plain. Seth Chagan Lal had interrupted his busy routine, busier no doubt by far now for having to deal as quickly as possible with the consequences of Dhartiraj having been removed from the role he had had in that deep-sucking investment of a film, in order to speak with him before his investigation had even begun to get under way. He had summoned him to warn him. But what exactly had that warning been of?

There had been all that talk of the amount of money involved, but not a word that was direct. Black money, could it be that? Everyone knew that films were often made with funds that were never put on paper for the tax man to see, money raised through smuggling and in half a dozen other illegal ways and converted through the profits of film-making into sums that could be used in the open. Stars too were often paid in black. Again that was something everybody knew. It was common gossip that they got two fees for everything, for signing a contract or as shares in a film's profits if they were high-enough ranking stars, one sum paid by cheque and entered in the books, the No. 1 money, and another, larger sum paid in cash, in huge wads of big hundred-rupee notes, the No. 2 money. Yet it was hard to see how the murder of Dhartiraj and some dubious black money transaction on the part of Seth Chagan Lal could be connected.

No, there must be something else which he had been warned about. He had been as good as told not to find out certain things, things that would add to the delays in making *Khoon Ka Gaddi*. But what exactly? What on earth could –

'Inspector.'

He blinked.

The Production Manager was standing at the foot of the

veranda steps, stumpy and bright-shirted as he had been a few minutes before. Why then did he seem so different? Why did everything seem changed, as if a whole new factor had been introduced into a situation that had seemed, just those few minutes earlier, crystal clear?

But whatever it was it would have to be thrust to the back of his mind now. He could not delay an instant longer. He had been on his way to the scene of the crime and it was there that he must go. And surely it was at that scene, among the simplicities of real and actual clues, that the path lay. There he could apply everything he had learnt over the years, the taking of statements, the making of measurements, the checking and the counter-checking. And from those the truth would emerge.

What had happened. And then the arrest under Section 201. And be damned to Seth Chagan Lal.

Yes, the Seth might be a great man in his own world. But here, in the police world, a star was rising in the heavens. His star. He had been put in charge of this case, this all-India important case. And he was going to bring someone to court at the end of it, charged with murder.

'Yes, Production Manager sahib,' he said. 'Take me to the scene of the crime.'

It was a tall corrugated-iron building standing at the very far end of the Studios compound with a high entrance door opening on long rails top and bottom. But this huge door had a small door within it, hardly five foot high and proportionately narrow. Above this a thin enamel notice-plate, streaked with rust, announced 'Sound Stage No. 2'.

'Inspector, it is here.'

The Production Manager pushed at the narrow door.

At once an angry voice bellowed out at them in sharp Marathi.

'No entry. No entry.'

The faintly stubbled face of a long-service police-constable appeared briefly in the sunlight.

'It is the CID Inspector. He has come.'

The constable stepped back at the Production Manager's

words and flicked up a salute. Ghote stooped a little and followed that orange shirt inside.

It was blackly dark. Partly this was the effect of stepping in out of the bright sun, but partly too it was due to a single very powerful light shining downwards somewhere in the middle of the tall building and cut off from them by tall screens reaching nearly up to the roof.

Scenery. Yes, of course, those would be scenery.

Ghote felt a renewed comforting sense of security at having known once again, almost instinctively, what was going on. He followed the bright orange shirt confidently into the thick dark, avoided neatly tripping over a great fat black cable snaking over the floor, succeeded in not knocking into any of the thin sloping struts supporting the scenery, and suddenly, with an effect of extravagant drama, found he had emerged into the pool of strong white light he had glimpsed above the tall scenery screens.

He might, he thought abruptly, be in some actual film. Under the glare of the light a rough circle of people, ranging from the most ordinary to the most extraordinary, stood unmoving as if caught for a still. A still, yes. That was the word.

It was at once plain which of the group was Director Ghosh, in charge of the shooting when Dhartiraj had been killed. It could only be that tall, swaying-bellied Bengali with the bold features and the long curling hair, dressed in a flowing white kurta and pyjama, a gold locket to be glimpsed hanging from a chain round his neck.

Next to him was a uniformed Assistant Inspector of Police, no doubt the fellow who had come in response to the first call made to the nearest police-station. Then the lanky chap standing next to the black, complicated-looking camera, which itself seemed one of the silent circle, must be the Cameraman who had been at work on the scene, a Gujerati by his looks.

But then, at the far side of the circle, was a face he recognized. A face indeed. A face in a million. Nilima. Nilima, a star of countless films, there herself. How often, though he was no cinema-goer, had he seen painted on hoardings those voluptuously beautiful features spread over almost a square yard of surface? Nilima, a legendary figure. Here, and standing struck as speechless as the rest of them.

Yes, and he would have to find out and quickly just who they all were. That fellow in the gorgeous red rajah's costume standing a little back from Nilima. He ought perhaps to know him too. Yet there was an odd downward-looking air to him that seemed very different from the radiating assurance of the star. Who would he be?

'Director sahib. It is the CID.'

At the Production Manager's words, spoken with a jarring loudness, Bhabani Ghosh had turned and stepped back a pace from the close circle. And the gap he made showed the sight they had all been standing silently looking down at, so many different forest animals hypnotized by a mighty snake. There, sprawled on the floor, harshly illuminated by that blinding white light, lay the heavy, red-robed body of a man. The murdered star.

Chapter 3

There was surprisingly little blood. A single dark rivulet ran congealed over the floor and a few heavy spots showed up on the white pages of two or three clipped-together sheets of paper lying nearby. More evident were the diamond-like fragments of glass scattered everywhere in thick pieces, debris from the big black lighting lamp whose fall must have been responsible for the star's death. It lay close against his shoulder, almost as if it had been propped up against a sleeping man.

It must, Ghote thought, have killed him at a stroke, probably snapping his neck as he had sat, leaning forwards, on the richly embroidered regal cushion just behind him.

But such matters would be for the police surgeon to decide. At this moment his information must come from the silent circle of onlookers.

He stepped forward and tersely introduced himself to the big Bengali director.

24

'You were here?' he asked. 'You saw what happened?'

Bhabani Ghosh looked at him with darkly brooding eyes.

'My God, Inspector,' he answered, 'I was directing him. Such a movie we were making.'

He lifted up his large head and stared into the distance. It seemed to Ghote that he must be very much aware how nearly his long locks resembled a lion's mane at that angle.

He put his next questions with considerable sharpness.

'You were directing him, telling him what to do? And then what? That big light fell? Did you look up? What exactly did you see? What did you see up there?'

He pointed to the blackness above.

Director Ghosh brought his gaze back to earth and blinked.

'Inspector,' he said, 'I saw nothing.'

'Nothing? Nothing? That light fell on your star, Mr Ghosh. How can you say you saw nothing?'

'Inspector, I was not there.'

'Not there? But you said – '

'Inspector, let me explain, I beg of you. Film business is a very complicated and difficult business, Inspector. It would not be possible for someone like you, an outsider only, to have any idea of what it is that happens.'

Ghote felt a faint chill stir in his mind. Was he after all bound to find himself always wandering in a strange country?

'Go on, Mr Ghosh,' he said, with a touch of grimness.

'Inspector, it was like this. Today I was able to have Dhartiraj for the morning shift. You understand the shift system, isn't it? We are having at present for *Khoon Ka Gaddi* an eight-day session of morning shifts. That is to say that for eight days I am able to film Dhartiraj from eight a.m. till twelve noon. At that time he goes to another studio shooting another film. I suppose he is – he was, I must say now – he was shooting at present some fifteen or sixteen films, and, of course, he has signed contracts for many more. Perhaps as many altogether as –

'But, excuse me.'

Ghote felt he had to interrupt. If he was not careful this word-torrenting Bengali would drown him in a huge lecture, a deluge of public facts. And the man behind them, the man who might have seen something vital to finding the killer of Dharti-raj, something even that he did not know that he had seen, might escape.

He interposed the first question that came to his mind to give himself time to think how best to get inside underneath the torrent.

'But, excuse me, to make a film in bits and pieces only, is that truly possible?'

And it seemed that this mere holding question had itself gone home under the gush. Bhabani Ghosh's expression of grand pourer-forth of impressive information disappeared from his large-featured face like steam blown away by a sharp chill wind. His big brown eyes looked directly at Ghote for the first time.

'Yes, Inspector,' he said, speaking now on a quiet note of intimacy. 'Yes, you have gone to the heart of it. It is impossible to make films, true films, in such conditions. You have heard of *Chaka*?'

Ghote had not, recognizing only that the word was Bengali for 'wheel'.

'No,' Bhabani Ghosh said with an underlying bitterness. 'Of course you have not heard of *Chaka*. It was only a true film, the story of a man's rise and inevitable decline. It was only my masterpiece.'

He smiled. A smile that was for himself.

'The film that I made,' he went on, 'before they asked me to forget I was a new-wave wallah and come to Bombay to make films that people would see, films using always a sneering Villain, a weeping mother, a bullying mother-in-law, stories with twin brothers parted in childhood or with fights on the cliff edge when the Hero wins against even a dozen *goondas* all wearing leather-jackets, backgrounds chosen because the studio had them on the film already. Yes, and I came. And I made these films. Twelve jubilees in five years, and one a gold.'

He glared down at Ghote. But Ghote knew that the animosity was not directed at him.

'Oh yes,' he went on in the same low intense tone, 'I made films that people would want to see, films with everything in

26

them all at once, films to make people dream they are living wicked Western ways – nightclubs and discos and all the time wearing jeans – and then to wake to find they are pure Hindus still. Yes, in bits and pieces I made such films.'

There was a glinting tear on one of his big flabby cheeks. And, Ghote thought, it is a tear not made of glycerine and placed with infinite care.

Glycerine. Where had he once read that this was how tears were produced in the film world? No matter where. He knew it. He knew more about this world than Director Ghosh had given him credit for. And he would find out whatever else he needed to know.

Now was the time, too. When he had got his witness looking at the truth.

'Please,' he said quietly. 'Please to tell me who were the people who actually saw Dhartiraj's death.'

'But I was explaining, Inspector. There was no one.'

'No one?'

He looked incredulously at the circle still gathered round the big red-robed recumbent body of the murdered star.

'Inspector,' Bhabani Ghosh said earnestly. 'By a curious chance there was in fact no one at all near Dhartiraj at the moment of his death. As I was telling, we were shooting this morning a scene where Dhartiraj, who is playing Raja Maqbet, was – '

'But – '

Ghote cursed himself for breaking in when the information was beginning to flow like this. But he could not help himself.

'But Dhartiraj is a great actor of Villains, isn't it?' he asked. 'And Macbeth is the Hero of Shakespeare's tragedy.'

Director Ghosh sighed.

'Oh, Inspector, Inspector,' he said, 'you have a lot to learn. You know Shakespeare's play?'

'Yes, yes.'

'Very well, in that Macbeth is killed in the end, isn't it? He is killed by Macduff. Now, do you think that anyone could make a Hindi film in which the Hero is killed? And by a side-hero only? No, no, the one who is left the winner must be the hero.

27

So in *Khoon Ka Gaddi* it is Maqduv who is the Hero, and he of course is played by the great Ravi Kumar himself. Dhartiraj was the Villain, Maqbet.'

'I see,' Ghote said.

'Very well.' The big Bengali resumed his explanation. 'The scene we were about to shoot was the one in which Maqbet seats himself upon the *gaddi* that he has wrongly usurped from Maqduv and – '

'But – No, no. Excuse me. Please go on.'

'Where Maqbet is seated upon the *gaddi* meditating upon the promise he has made to his mother that he will not harm Maqduv, the son she has borne out of wedlock, only as it will come out in the end it is Maqbet who was born out of wedlock and Maqduv who is the rightful rajah.'

'I see.'

'Well now, I had gone through the dialogues for this with Dhartiraj and we had agreed at what moment he was to rise to his feet and beat at his breast. So it was next a question of the lighting, and for that I was using a stand-in. But when the fellow comes he is wearing the turban that Dhartiraj himself will wear in the shooting, and as soon as Dhartiraj saw it he realized that there was something altogether wrong. It had not nearly enough jewels for an artiste of Dhartiraj's stature, that is to say for a rajah of the stature of Maqbet.'

'Yes, yes, I see.'

'Very well. So Dhartiraj sent the stand-in to obtain more jewels from the Property Department, and in the meanwhile he sat down on the *gaddi* to go through his dialogues while I went out of the set to have discussions with my Cameraman where – '

'Bhabaniji, Bhabaniji. Director of Photography, if you please.'

It was the Gujerati beside the craning-forward camera who had been listening with avidity to every word the Director had been saying.

Bhabani Ghosh's bold features took on a look of swift contempt.

'Very well, I went into conference with my Director of Photography about what orders it would be necessary to give the

28

Lights Boys. You know that each light is operated by a coolie up on a catwalk?'

'Yes, yes,' said Ghote, who had not known.

'Very well, so Chandubhai there and his assistants came with me and the Audiographer also, what you would be calling the sound man.'

'I see.'

'And Dhartiraj's make-up man, knowing it was too soon to correct his make-up, went to the canteen, leaving Dhartiraj alone on the set.'

Ghote thought he had grasped the situation.

'And then?' he asked.

'Then? Then, quite soon after we had begun our conference, there was, I am almost sure, a sudden whistling sound and the Five-K came – '

'Excuse me, the Five-K?'

'The five-kilowatt light,' Director Ghosh explained, a little testily. 'We are using a great number of different lights for different purposes in filming, Five-Ks, Two-Ks, Sunspots, Solars, Babies. But, as I was trying to tell, I am almost certain that I actually heard the whistle of that light coming down. And then there was a sickening crash. Perhaps one moan only from Dhartiraj. And silence.'

'Silence. Then what?'

'Why, then we all rushed back to the set and saw just what you yourself can see now. Believe me, Inspector, I at once ordered that nothing, but nothing, was to be moved. The thought that it was an accident for which the Studios might be blamed was the first thing that came into my head. And at once I sent a Lights Boy up to see what had happened up there, and to report to me personally. If it had been a rope that had frayed, then it was important to hide – Then it was important to keep the evidence, you understand.'

'I understand. But it cannot have been a frayed rope that the Lights Boy reported.'

'No, it was not,' Bhabani Ghosh said sombrely. 'He told me that the ropes holding the Five-K had been severed. Cut clean through with an abominably sharp knife.'

'And that was when you knew it was murder and telephoned for the police?'

'Yes, yes. And in double quick time this gentleman here, Assistant Inspector – Assistant Inspectorji, I was never hearing your name.'

The Assistant Inspector clicked his heels.

'Assistant Inspector Jahdev.'

'You arrived on the scene at what time, A I?' Ghote asked.

'Ten thirty-seven ack emma, Inspector.

'And at what time did the light fall?' Ghote asked Bhabani Ghosh.

'I was altogether too overwhelmed to note the time, Inspector. But it cannot have been longer than fifteen minutes before Mr – er – Mr Jahdev arrived.'

So, Ghote thought, there was every chance that nothing material had been altered. He could see the circumstances just as they had been at the moment someone had cut those ropes, watched the Five-K – yes, the Five-K – crash down on to Dhartiraj and had then slipped away in the darkness up above.

But that someone had a body. He was not the invisible man. He must have climbed up to that catwalk immediately above the set and have hurried down again. He had not been seen up there, but the chances were that he had been seen elsewhere although plainly no one here had spotted anybody running from the scene.

Questioning, thorough and precise questioning, might well make it absolutely clear however that someone was unaccounted for. The someone.

It would be a matter of hammering at them all. Of forcing from people's minds things they did not know were there. And he would do it.

He turned back to Bhabani Ghosh.

'You were telling that you were about to arrange the lighting for the scene of Dhartiraj meditating upon the *gaddi*,' he said. 'And you said also that each light up there has a Lights Boy to look after it. How many of them were up with their lights then? Where are they now?'

Too frightened to talk. If he knew anything.

'But no, Inspector,' the Director said. 'For this scene I intended to have one spotlight only. Maqbet was to be haloed in light. It was an effect I had used in my *Chaka.*'

For a moment a look almost of desolation came into his eyes. But he hurried on.

'So, you see, there was no one on the catwalk directly above the set. Indeed, all the Lights Boys had gone to the canteen. And the single light we were using had the effect of making everything up there even more dark than usual.'

'I see. So it would not have been at all difficult for the person who cut those ropes to do so unobserved?'

'Exactly, Inspector.'

There was a note of sombre satisfaction in the tall Bengali's voice. The very impenetrability of the affair seemed to give him deep pleasure.

Ghote felt a sharp surge of white-hot determination.

'Nothing could be seen up there?' he barked.

'Nothing, Inspector.'

'Nothing from down here perhaps,' he came banging back. 'But what about the one light that was on? And the lights coolie for that? He was up there. What did he see?'

Inside him a fountain of brightness spurted high at Director Ghosh's instant look of acknowledgement. No, the Deputy Commissioner had chosen well. A new bright light was needed to shine into the darkness the *filmi* people delighted to wrap round themselves. And he was it. Despite every doubt, he felt it now. A new light to penetrate that dark.

Chapter 4

An unexpected intrusion, however, prevented Ghote getting at once to the lights coolie who might well turn out to have seen, not the man who had cut the ropes of the Five-K above Dhartiraj's head, but something, even some already forgotten tiny incident, that could put him firmly on the trail of the murderer.

31

He was, in fact, a little delayed by the arrival of the rest of the team from Headquarters, the men from the Fingerprint Bureau, a photographer, a stretcher party to take the body away eventually to the police surgeon. But it was while he was dealing with them, his determination kept just beneath the surface like a powerful film-studio light itself ready at a flick to throw the whole of his life into a new brilliant brightness, that the real interruption occurred.

The Bombay corps of Press reporters came clamouring loudly to the sound-stage door.

He decided it was his bounden duty to see them. After all, this was no ordinary crime. A star had been murdered. A man known to millions all over India. It was right that the investigator himself should tell the world what there was to be told.

He held his conference just outside the big studio, discovering as he stepped out that the sun had mercifully gone behind a big sailing white cloud so that there was no reason not to stand out where they were.

Some twenty or more reporters were gathered there and for almost half an hour they banged question after question at him. He had never before experienced an encounter with the Press at this pitch and he was bitterly conscious that on occasions he floundered.

There was even one moment when he was reduced to prolonged and hopeless silence.

It came just after he had dealt particularly well with a query from a man with whom he had had talks more than once in the past, the crime reporter of the *Free Press*. He had asked the sort of question that he himself felt ought to be put, a simple request to know exactly what forces the CID were devoting to the case, and it had not been difficult to produce in reply an impressive list of almost every facility they had, right down to naming the police dogs who might possibly be of use, Caesar, Akbar, Moti. Then, a tall beaky-nosed woman at the back, whom he had not previously noticed, an angular creature in a sari of tiny green squares, abruptly called out.

'Miss Pilloo Officewalla, chief gossip writer *Film Femme*. If your investigations should lead you to believe a famous star has murdered Dhartiraj out of mad jealousy, what steps would you take?'

It was not that it was difficult to answer. It was simply that he could not believe what he had heard. And for second after second he had stood there mentally repeating the words.

Miss Officewalla, whom he discovered to his surprise when he mentioned her afterwards to his *Free Press* acquaintance was considered to be Queen of the Gossip Writers, had actually begun to put the whole question again before he banged the only possible reply.

'Madam, if I had arrived at such a conclusion I would proceed to arrest the gentleman in question.'

'Or lady?' Miss Officewalla shot out.

Again he felt a sensation of obliterating bewilderment. What world was this that he had entered?

But he managed to reply more speedily.

'Is it likely, madam, that a lady would be involved? You have heard me outline the circumstances of the crime.'

One of the reporters at the front did then ask, plainly only out of a sense of duty, whether he did in fact have reason to suspect a male star and no one had seemed disappointed when he had reminded them that he had been at the Studios for less than an hour. And then someone asked something which gave him a splendid final chance of expressing his determination 'to solve this beastly crime with all possible speed and to see that justice is meted out to the person, or persons, wherever they have chosen to hide themselves, who have done to death such a star as the late and the great and the greatly lamented Dhartiraj'. And how the pencils had raced across the titled notebooks at that.

It was a rich moment. And there would be others for the man who had cracked the Dhartiraj case. They would crowd round him, the reporters, in the years to come just as they crowded round the stars of the *filmi duniya*.

But they were leaving now, hurrying away to telephones and typewriters, and he turned to the sway-bellied figure of Bhabani Ghosh.

'Now, what about the coolie who was up on the catwalks – it is catwalks, isn't it? – at the time the Five-K fell?'

'Yes, Inspector. It is old Ailoo. He is our oldest Lights Boy. He was actually the fellow I sent up to see whether the ropes had frayed, an altogether reliable fellow.'

They went back in and once more Ghote threaded his way through the thick darkness of the big studio. He stopped when they reached the throne-room set again to make a rapid check on the Headquarters technicians at work there. It was important to show them that there was someone in charge who was right on top of every least thing. Then he set off following the tall white-muslin-clad back of Director Ghosh, along narrow corridors formed by the tall canvas frames of other sets, peering hard in the faint illumination that came from two or three low-powered bulbs high in the ceiling of the tall building. Glimpses of strange, over-bright scenes caught his eye, a paddy-field painted on a wall stretching back in row after row of neat cones of rice-straw, a prison-cell composed only of a wall of metal-painted wooden bars. It was stuffily hot, with the occasional huge fan standing idle.

And at last they came to the rough representation of a country drinking-shop, a black-doored hut with a crudely carved table and bench outside it, dotted with squat bottles.

'Where Maqbet and Banko discuss the witches they have seen,' Bhabani Ghosh explained.

Ducking under the green-paper branches of a squat palm-tree, Ghote felt a small jab of pleasure that at least the witches had been left in Shakespeare's play by – what was his name? – yes, by Dr Avind Bhatt, Litt.D.

But it was the man sitting on the ground, his back resting against the canvas wall of the drinking-shop, who claimed his attention. He did not need the Director's murmured 'This is old Ailoo' to tell him that the gaunt figure – he must have been anything between fifty and seventy with short-cropped grey hair and a grey stubble on his lean face – wearing only a pair of tattered khaki shorts was the person he wanted.

He had scrambled to his feet at Director Ghosh's words and the moment that the tall Bengali left them Ghote tackled him.

'Now, you were the Lights Boy operating the only light that was being used for the scene of Dhartiraj upon the *gaddi*?'

'Yes, Inspector sahib. Light No. 12, Inspector sahib.'

Well, at least the fellow seeemed intelligent.

'Good. Now, I want you to tell me exactly what you saw over in the darkness above where Dhartiraj was. Exactly, mind.'

'Sahib, I did not see.'

Rage spewed up inside him, sudden and overwhelming. To meet with stupid obstinacy now. He did not deserve that.

'What do you mean you did not see?' he shouted. 'You were there, isn't it? Up there on the catwalks? And there was some-one else up there too, not so very far away. How dare you say you saw nothing?'

'Sahib, I saw nothing.'

Ghote raised his hand to bring the taut palm slapping down across the old man's face.

Old Ailoo stood there, impassively waiting to receive the blow. And at the last moment Ghote checked himself.

This was not the way to deal with a witness. It was not the way he had dealt with witnesses in other investigations. He must not allow the overwhelming importance of this case, those whis-perings of the great things that would come from it, to make him forget himself. For better or worse, he had always tried never to lose his temper except in pretence during an interrog-ation. And he must stick to that.

'Come,' he said to the old man, 'you and I have much to talk. This is not the place. Where can we go where we would be more comfortable?'

Old Ailoo's grey-stubbled face lost none of the calm accept-ance with which he had awaited the blow.

'Sahib,' he said, after a moment's grave consideration, 'there is Recording Room. It is very small, sahib, but it is air-con-ditioned. And since there is no more shooting it would not be in use.'

'Good idea,' Ghote said. 'First-class idea. Show me the way.'

The old coolie did not react to this praise in the way he had hoped. But nevertheless he set off at a good pace into the mys-terious darkness of the huge studio. Ghote followed his spine-jutting back past painted village – there was a well, looking exactly like the one he had known in boyhood, wide and friendly, but when he idly touched one of its grey stones it proved to be no more than hollow plaster-of-paris – past prison cell, past grimy city wall, until they came to the Recording Room.

This turned out to be no more than a largish grey-painted booth filled with various pieces of apparatus, all dials and knobs. But it was certainly pleasantly cool after the musty heat of the big studio. Ghote moved a pair of headphones and sat himself on the Audiographer's stool and old Ailoo stood, at as respectful a distance as the little booth permitted.

'Well now,' Ghote began again, 'you say that, although you were up on the catwalk beside your light – Light No. 12, wasn't it? – you did not see anything or anybody over the place where Dhartiraj was killed. Tell me, how did that come to be?'

'Sahib, it is very easy. I was working the light.'

'But no,' Ghote said. 'Surely not. Director Ghosh was discussing still what exact lighting to use. There was nothing for you to be busy over.'

'Sahib, no. It is much more than that. When you are at your light it is what you are doing. You must always be ready. Ready for the sahibs to call up "Tilt left, No. 12. Tilt right. Pan up, pan down. Make harder, make softer. Silk diffuser, quickly, quickly. No, glass diffuser, you idiot." '

Old Ailoo reproduced the words, no doubt daily shouted to him, without the least trace of resentment. And Ghote got a sudden glimpse of the life he must lead up on the catwalks, with the world below reduced to voices bawling up at him to make his light do this or that as if he were no more than a piece of machinery. And there would be a precariousness, too, about his existence. The catwalks he had glanced up at as he had threaded his way here and there through the fantastic world of the studio had looked appallingly narrow, two planks wide only, sometimes one, secured with tangled lengths of frayed-out rope, swooping and swaying all across the high roof of the huge building. Did coolies ever fall?

He put the question to old Ailoo.

'Oh yes, sahib. Light Boys falling from catwalk sometimes. We had one in this very studio who broke his back, not one month ago. He was moving a Baby. You know what is a Baby, sahib?'

'Yes, yes. Well I am knowing such things.'

'Yes, sahib. Well, when Benwa had untied the rope of the Baby it slipped from his hand as he was moving, sahib. He swung out to catch and he fell. In hospital still, sahib, and what is his wife to do and his four children?'

Ailoo stopped abruptly, seemingly feeling that he must have said too much. Ghote quickly sought for another question to ask. If he could get the old man to talk freely he might yet remember something he had half-seen in the darkness when that Five-K had been cut down.

'Lights falling like that, is that something that happens often?'

'No, no, sahib. Not so often as coolies falling. Lights very-very costly, sahib.'

Again old Ailoo relapsed into uncomplaining silence.

'Was anyone else hurt when that Baby fell?' Ghote asked, determined to keep this forthcoming vein of talk alive.

'There had been a man almost underneath,' Ailoo resumed. 'A stand-in wallah called Sudhaker Wani. But Benwa had called out, so he was not truly in danger even though afterwards he cursed him as if he had done that on purpose.'

'He ought to have been grateful,' Ghote contributed.

'Oh, but he is a terrible fellow, that one. Always doing things to get himself money, fetching and carrying and obtaining for whoever will pay.'

The old man's disgust at a way of life so different from his own single-minded devotion to his light was almost laughable.

'But the Baby that so nearly killed him,' Ghote asked now, glimpsing a way of bringing the talk round to what he wanted to know. 'It was purely an accident that it fell?'

'Oh yes, sahib. Benwa is a good and careful fellow. That day in the studio it was very-very hot and he was sweating very much. That is why the Baby slipped.'

'I see. But the Five-K today, that was a different matter, eh?'

'Oh yes, altogether, Inspector. Those ropes had been cut.'

'How many ropes?'

'Two. Two only, Inspector.'

'Two quick cuts, and then the Five-K would fall straight on to Dhartiraj?'

Old Ailoo looked at him with an expression of the utmost seriousness.

'Inspector, I am certain of that. Certain.'

'So someone cut them,' Ghote said softly. 'Someone did that. And did you see nothing of them?'

'Sahib, no.'

'Not a glimpse of the colour of a shirt? Not the whisk of the tail of a *dhoti*?'

'Inspector, I wish with all my heart that there had been.'

The old man laid a thin work-scarred hand on the ribby cage of his chest.

And Ghote believed him. What he had said rang true. He was one of life's truly simple people. He had his job. He did it. He had no aspirations beyond what that job called for. No glancing always elsewhere for him to see if a better chance was to be grabbed. No, he had seen nothing.

'There is just the question of access,' he said to him at last.

'Access, sahib?'

'Of the way the man we want could have got up to the cat-walk above Dhartiraj.'

'Oh, that is quite easy, sahib. There are iron ladders here and there round the walls of the studio, and that is how we get up to our places. The one for the catwalk over Dhartiraj would be the one in the corner nearest the big door.'

'Would it be easy for someone to get up unseen by that one?'

Old Ailoo thought carefully.

'Yes. Yes, sahib, it would. That ladder is in a very dark corner with the sets they are having just now. Unless someone was standing there, and there is no reason for anyone to do that, it would be altogether easy to climb up with no one seeing.'

Ghote pursed his lips.

'But that is not the ladder for your place, for Light No. 12?' he asked.

'No, no, sahib. Mine is the next ladder along. The two cat-walks are not joined together at all. You would have to go down and up again to get from my place to that one. So I did not kill him, sahib.'

The old man was completely unresentful of the accusation he had heard in Ghote's question.

'You can swing across on a rope, sahib,' he added in the same placid tone. 'But only a young fool would do that. It is danger-ous, and there is no need.'

'I see,' Ghote said.

He sat in silence reviewing all that he had learnt. And the more he thought the more certain he became that the situation was by no means as simple as he had hoped when it had oc-curred to him that someone working Light No. 12 should have at least glimpsed something of the man who had cut the Five-K's ropes.

'No,' he said at last, 'I do not think there is anything more I have to ask you, Ailoo. I had hoped you would have seen some-thing. But I see now that you did not. No, strange as it may seem, I really believe no one at all saw whoever was up there.'

He sighed.

'So it looks as though I shall have to go about my business another way,' he said. 'A longer and harder way.'

Chapter 5

It was while Inspector Ghote was up on the narrow and sway-ing catwalk examining for himself the Five-K's two sliced-through ropes that he fastened on his decision. It was a decision which had lurked under everything he had done since question-ing old Ailoo had proved that, for all the number of people inside the No. 2 Sound Stage at the moment Dhartiraj had been done to death – and he had had an almost panoramic view of them all by the time he had climbed three-quarters of the way up the ladder – it was almost certain that there had been no one who had seen the murderer.

He had climbed up with Assistant Inspector Jahdev – a fellow, it had turned out, of an almost impossible talkativeness, once freed from the constraints of mingling with *filmi* people – and all the while that he had listened at interminable length to explanations of every step that had already been taken and every step it was intended to take in the primary investigation to which his own inquiries were, in the official word, 'parallel' he had been aware dully that the case would now be a question, not of the almost instant triumph which such a dramatic murder seemed to call for, but of days and even weeks of patient exploration of the dead star's life. It would be a matter of unearthing any motive which anybody close to the star might have. It might all too easily peter out in a tangled mass of vague possibilities and there would never be that dazzling moment when the prosecution would call its chief witness and he himself would step into the box, a star, to tell the world how he had tracked down a star's murderer.

So at last he had made up his mind to it.

'A I,' he had said, breaking in on a dissertation on the various types of knots that could be made with ropes, 'I suggest that you go at once and find Miss Pilloo Officewalla, chief gossip writer of *Film Femme*, if she is still in the Studios. I would like to pick her brains on this *filmi duniya*.'

But, waiting in the Production Manager's cabin which he had managed to secure for his own use, for the arrival of Miss Officewalla, he could not help experiencing a certain trepidation, despite the sheer fantasy of the question she had put to him at the Press conference. The beaky-nosed gossip writer represented, he felt, all the unknown and even unknowable complexities of the *filmi duniya*. She was, if what he had learnt of her was only half true, in her own person the high priestess of a world that seemed to be conducted on entirely different principles from his own everyday existence. And, besides, those questions of hers had been put with a terrible sharpness.

How he would have liked to have done what he had planned while he was still on his way to the Studios, to have visited the shop of some *raddiwallah* and have bought from his store of old newspapers acquired at one-third of their published price a good pile of film magazines from which he could have extracted at leisure a whole background of knowledge. It was the sort of work he liked best. To be tucked away steadily amassing knowledge, working through quantities of material that might be dull but were yet pregnant with the possibility of some startling result.

But such a slow but steady method was no longer right. If he was to bring the murderer of Dhartiraj to justice as quickly as his thousands of fans would require, then he must act with speed. And for that it would be necessary to secure the total collaboration of Miss Pilloo Officewalla.

The constable whom Assistant Inspector Jahdev had placed on duty outside tapped loudly at the door.

This is it, he thought.

'Come in, please. Who is it?'

As if he did not know.

The door was held open. Miss Officewalla, tall, her softly green sari swishing silkily, her big thin beaky nose preceding her, entered.

He asked her to sit. He offered tea. He accepted its refusal. Briefly as he could he explained his needs.

'Well, you have come to the right person, Inspector,' she said, leaning forward across the desk that separated them until it seemed her nose was about to dip experimentally into the piles of papers he had collected.

'Yes,' she went on, *'Film Femme* gossip is the best in India, though I am saying it. Who exposed the cleavage photos scandal? Who was first with the news of Kundan's midnight decision to marry? Who, and who only, had the full story of Nilima's life from her earliest moments balanced as a baby on a tall bamboo already earning her keep in her simple entertainers' family to stardom and her torrid affair with Ravi Kumar? Who first – '

Ghote held up his hands to stem the flood.

'Miss Officewalla, I am thoroughly knowing your achievements in journalism line,' he lied. 'But it is incumbent upon me now to proceed with minimum waste of time. Assistant Inspector Jahdev is preparing for me a list of all those who might have connection with the late Dhartiraj who were in the compound here at the time of the crime. But doubtless you already know many of those names. What I am asking is that you should go through them making whatever frank comments you like. In that way I may learn what motives people could have for ending Dhartiraj's life.'

Miss Officewalla shook her narrow head.

'Ah, Inspector, I see that you do not at all know the *filmi duniya*,' she said.

Ghote felt affronted. After having lied so neatly about her journalistic achievements it seemed quite unfair to be told promptly that he knew nothing of the film world.

'No, Inspector,' Miss Officewalla went on. 'This is the whole point about Dhartiraj. He was the star without an enemy. He was a kind man to everybody, always ready to be Chief Guest at a charity show or to make a Friendly Appearance in another star's film. He was the universally loved member of the *filmi* community. A happy man always, bluff and hearty in every way. No one in all the time he has been a star ever accused that man of creating mutual rifts and tensions. Except, of course, Ravi Kumar.'

'But – '

Ghote bit the question back. Ravi Kumar was, after all, the No. 1 Superstar and it would show appalling ignorance not to know why he, of course, was the only person who would ever have accused Dhartiraj of creating rifts and tensions.

But, luckily, it appeared that the Ravi Kumar–Dhartiraj clash was another of Miss Officewalla's particular triumphs. Without being asked, she proceeded to enlighten him.

So he listened, patiently as he could, while she unfolded her long tale. Ravi Kumar, it seemed, had years ago taken Dhartiraj's wife from him. And ever since he had refused to have Dhartiraj in any film with him – what pride the fellow must have, Ghote thought, when it was he who was in the wrong. But it had been Miss Officewalla, and Miss Officewalla alone, who had learnt that Seth Chagan Lal had when casting *Khoon Ka Gaddi* at last persuaded the Superstar to relent.

He longed all the while to get back to matters that were

relevant to the case. But he no longer dared interrupt. He had begun to feel that if he was to be a star investigator, then, should he once betray ignorance of the film stars' world, luck would instantly repay him by withholding some vital fact he would need to get his man.

'And who,' Miss Officewalla demanded suddenly, 'was the first to print that Ravi Kumar had lost his keep?'

'Keep?' he asked, at once betraying his new resolution almost before it had been formed.

But it seemed Miss Officewalla was prepared to condone a degree of ignorance for the sake of the full retailing of such an extraordinary professional success. Perhaps fate would be as kind.

'Keep? Keep is the old joke, Inspector. What does a Producer get when he has his first hit film? A jeep and a keep.'

She leant forward and her beaky nose twitched.

'A keep. A mistress.'

'Oh yes. Yes, of course,' Ghote said hurriedly.

'What a story,' Miss Officewalla went happily on. 'To have your latest keep stolen from you by the very man whose wife you had stolen in the first place. And then she too, that little Meena, was in the film at that time.'

Suddenly the implications of what she had been saying struck home to Ghote. Was she not laying out, when you came down to it, a classic motive for murder?

'Please,' he interrupted. 'Please, tell me more about this Miss Meena. She is a star?'

He made no effort now to pretend that he already knew.

'A *bachchi* star, yes,' Miss Officewalla said. 'She had not yet taken any role, but she had been cast as the Rani Maqbet in *Khoon Ka Gaddi*. Of course, this was the influence of Ravi Kumar. The girl was a Decent Extra only when he took her. But as his mistress she naturally had a chance of stardom. And she would – '

'Excuse me.'

Ghote felt that once again he had to break in. It was worth any loss of esteem to get all the details of this quite clear.

From behind Miss Officewalla's beak of a nose a look of

brief contempt did appear now. But she paused to explain.

'A Decent Extra is an extra of the class that can be used in top society scenes, as guests in nightclubs, that sort of thing. They have decent clothes they can wear, a suit or a sari of something more than cotton. Though they are often extremely flashy.'

She glanced down at her own sari with its subdued pattern of small green squares.

'They would be paid at the rate of Rupees 25 a day,' she went on. 'Instead of the Rupees 100 per mensem that the ordinary extra would be pulling down.'

'Yes,' said Ghote. 'Thank you.'

'Now, as I was telling. That Meena – heaven knows what her name was originally – although she was a *bachchi* star only, was also altogether a sex-bomb. At parties she would wear her sari so low that it revealed not only the navel but the beginning of the curve of the buttocks also as if she was all the time playing the Vamp in a film.'

Miss Officewalla looked severe.

'So of course,' she went on, 'the girl was beginning to make a name for herself. *Film Femme* had to recognize her with a cover. Even established stars were having to take notice of her so as not to be accused of jealousy. We ourselves had a very good photo of her being offered a glass of cane-juice by Nilima herself. She was altogether rising fast in the estimation of the fans.'

Ghote felt puzzled still as to how this could be when the girl had not yet even been seen on the screen. But he decided he had better not put forward this view.

'Yes, yes,' he murmured encouragingly.

'Yes, she would have done very well, even though she did not know acting, if it had not been for her so-called illness.'

Miss Officewalla put such meaning into the last words that Ghote felt obliged to say 'Ah ha' as significantly as he could.

'The illness,' Miss Officewalla triumphantly added, 'that, as I said and said in my page, was no more than the simple effect of the strain upon her love loyalties.'

'Ah,' Ghote repeated, though he felt himself to be sadly floundering.

'Yes, yes. Although they continued to put out medical reports that the girl had wasted away from some disease, they were never able to put a name to it at all. And the fact remains that soon after she had given up the role of Rani Maqbet, because she had got too thin to be a star, she left Ravi Kumar to go to Dhartiraj. My revelation she had done that was the greatest sensation ever to come out of Bollywood.'

'Bollywood?' Ghote asked, experiencing yet another surge of bewilderment.

Miss Officewalla's thin face sharpened instantly into a totally scandalized look.

'Do you not read at all, Inspector?' she demanded. 'The Bombay film set-up is called Bollywood in simply every film magazine. I had thought that Crime Branch CID were at least educated.'

That had been a bad moment. But Ghote, though shot through with darts of despair at the thought of how much admitting such ignorance would have turned luck against him, would not let himself abandon the prickly business of learning from Miss Officewalla every bit he could about the *filmi duniya*. His grim determination had been reinforced by her brisk dismissal of his interest in Ravi Kumar. The superstar, she had said witheringly, could not possibly have been inside the Talkiestan Studios compound. A superstar did not go about anywhere unnoticed, least of all at the gates of film studios.

He had sent out to Assistant Inspector Jahdev to check on this, but he had known that it was a vain hope. And so it had proved. Assistant Inspector Jahdev had brought in his list of all the people known to be within the high walls and guarded gate of the Talkiestan compound at the time Dhartiraj had been killed, and of course the name of Ravi Kumar was not among them.

So bit by bit he had extracted from the gossip queen a few names of those in some way close to Dhartiraj optimistically to put down on a large sheet of paper he had headed 'People to

See'. There was the star's personal pandit (but he was a notoriously saintly and very aged astrologer). There was his personal make-up man (but he had been with the star for years and was well-known as his chosen confidant, even if he was also, as it emerged, in Miss Officewalla's pay). There was his secretary (but she was new to the job, and it was certain that Dhartiraj, busy with his new keep, had not made any advances of a sexual nature to her). There was his former secretary (but she was newly and happily married to an account executive). There was his personal assistant (but he too was tried and trusted, though not in the pay of Miss Officewalla but in that of one of her rivals, even if what he told her was 'not at all reliable'). There were his *chumchas*.

'*Chumchas?*' Ghote asked.

He knew that the word meant 'spoons' in Hindi, but he could not, put to it, exactly produce its *filmi duniya* meaning. *Chumchas* were something to do with stars, but what?

The look of sheer disapproval returned to Miss Officewalla's face – Ghote felt that at any moment he might feel the sharp peck of her nose-beak – but she answered his question. In an icily chilled voice.

'A *chumcha* is the follower of a star. He feeds his star with whatever he is needing, laughter for his jokes, praise for his performances, revelations on his rivals and scorn for the gossip writers. And in return the star feeds him, with food at the posh hotels of Juhu, with drink from his bar, with a small part in a film sometimes. And they vie who can serve him best, make him laugh the most, however ridiculous they have to make themselves, find him the best girl, tell him the dirtiest stories.'

'Yes, yes,' Ghote said rapidly. 'All this I am of course well knowing, though it is kind of you to remind. But what I am wanting to find out is: would not one of these fellows very likely bear a grudge against Dhartiraj? What are the names of Dhartiraj's *chumchas*, if you please?'

He poised his ballpoint, which only then did he notice was an altogether unsatisfactory shade of bright pink.

'It is of no use,' Miss Officewalla briskly replied. 'You see, his *chumchas* –'

But he felt he had to reassert his authority now, the authority of the CID's top investigator.

'Please, madam, the names. I require.'

Miss Officewalla heaved a sigh.

'Very well. Khwaja Abbas, Khrishan Chander, Jayawant Dalvi, Suresh Joshi, Adil Jussawalla, Manohar Malgonkar, Ashok Mitran, Mangat Rai, Partap Sharma, Baldev Vaid. And I suppose you might put in with them, young Kishore Sachdev.'

Ghote scribbled, recognizing that to produce such a list in one long breath, and in alphabetical order too, was tremendous confirmation of Miss Officewalla's command of her profession.

'Kishore Sachdev?' he asked, at last looking up.

'Oh, he is a well-off boy Dhartiraj brought from Delhi to try his luck in films after he had met him two-three years ago at the big Stars Charity Cricket Match. You know, the time Billy Banker went on the field dressed as a Western ballet girl.'

She gave him a sharp look.

'Billy Banker is a famous comedian,' she added.

'Yes, yes, I am knowing.'

Ghote felt the sting. Everybody knew Billy Banker, perpetual broadly grinning joker on and off the screen.

He glared down at his list of names.

'Very well,' he said. 'I will investigate each and every one of these fellows. And pretty thoroughly, I can tell you.'

'But, Inspector,' Miss Officewalla said, cool as ever. 'It would be of no use. I was explaining. Each of those people depends entirely on Dhartiraj. Some he was buying from other stars even. Any he could sell, though he did not. It would be killing the golden goose altogether for them to attempt to murder him.'

He looked at her with suspicion.

'You are certain?'

'Inspector, I have my reputation. You can check easily. Any one of my rivals would confirm.'

'Well . . .'

He was unhappy to let them go. They had extended his roll-call of possibilities marvellously.

'But these other names you have given me,' he said, feeling a definite sense of grievance. 'None of them is exactly a one hundred per cent possibility.'

To his surprise Miss Officewalla looked abruptly irritated.

'That I am giving?' she said. 'But I am not at all giving. It is you who have been asking. If you are wanting my advice, that is another matter altogether.'

He looked up.

'You have advice? There is someone you believe might have killed Dhartiraj? Someone who was here?'

'Inspector, am I to get your maximum full co-operation?'

'Yes, Miss Officewalla,' he said.

There seemed to be no other reply he could make. A No. 1 investigator had to get results with No. 1 swiftness. And so far he was getting nowhere at all.

Miss Officewalla drew herself up and looked at him hard down her beaky nose.

'Jagdish Rana,' she said.

'Jagdish Rana, he is a star. Yes, he is a star.'

A bright little flame of triumph sang in him. Jagdish Rana was a name he knew of old, one that he had seen on posters and in advertisements by the hundred here and there about Bombay over the years.

'Yes, even you would know him,' Miss Officewalla said. 'Until four or five years back Hari Ram – as he was called at birth – was a really sizeable marquee name, one you would see on the front of half-a-dozen cinemas at a time. He was the Villain in every film there was, hit picture or flop picture. Until Dhartiraj came from nowhere and toppled him from his place.'

Was that motive enough? Ghote's first instinct was to reject it as nonsense. But then the weight of all the various things he had been learning in this long, long morning about the way of the *filmi duniya* came home to him. No. No, perhaps to be toppled like that was motive enough for murder, in this world.

'Yes,' said Miss Officewalla, seeing the thought harden in his eyes, 'he had reason to hate Dhartiraj all right. Dhartiraj who was a Punjabi just like him, Dhartiraj who had reduced him to playing side heroes only, like Banko in *Khoon Ka Gaddi* and lucky even to get that. Dhartiraj who was on the point of pushing him out from being a star altogether. Inspector, if I were you I would go at once and talk to Jagdish Rana.'

Chapter 6

Ghote was at the studio gates on his way to the beach at Juhu where, so Miss Officewalla had told him, Jagdish Rana, the fading star, was shooting on location, when the Pathan chowki-dar came running up. He thrust his fanciful turban in at the car window, bringing with him a blast of highly spiced breath that made him realize that he had gone without a midday meal himself.

'Inspector,' he said, 'we had orders not to let you leave the Studios.'

'What is this?'

The fellow cleared his throat with a tremendous solemn rat-tling.

'Sahib, it is Miss Nilima. She is wishing to see you.'

He spoke with awe. And Ghote in his turn experienced much the same feeling.

Nilima, the great star. Even as infrequent a cinema-goer as he was, he had seen Nilima on the wide silver screen at least some dozen times over the years. A distant figure of marvellous beauty, of charged sexuality, a dream. True, she had never obsessed him as in sober fact she obsessed the thoughts of thou-sands and thousands of men all over India. But there had been moments, watching her in enormous close-up from far away across the dark spaces of a cinema, and able to examine her as he never could have examined anyone like her in reality, when certain thoughts had lodged for a little in his mind.

She was, after all, exceptional. Her figure had a fullness rare to see in such perfection, and was always seen to the utmost advantage. Soft saris clung caressingly to her hips. Or, portray-ing some simple Rajasthani peasant girl in *ghagra* and *choli*, the latter was always at stitch-straining point across her bosom. Or, wearing Western clothes, her shirt was so low-buttoned that it

49

looked as if at every instant the last rules of decency were to be burst apart. Her face, too, was composed of everything that might rouse the sensual, a seemingly flawless skin of infinite touchability, poutingly full lips, enormous melting eyes, a continuous teasing play of expression.

And she had summoned him to see her. Why? Impossible to tell. Except that – the thought came to him late – he was now, suddenly, lifted up, a person who could talk to Nilima, with any other star of the high world of the films.

But, if he was such an investigator, ought he not to be going out to crack this case, to bust it wide open? Should he obey the summons?

A battle raged within him.

It was decided only by the look of total assurance on the fierce sweat-streaked face thrust in at the car window. If it was so much assumed that he would at once go to Nilima, then had he not better go?

And, besides, he could deal with whatever business it was she wanted to consult him over in double-quick time. That would be the way, yes.

With the tall turbaned Pathan loping along at his vehicle's wing, they went once more through the crowded confusion of the Studios compound – a little less excited now, a little more purposeful – until they came to Sound Stage No. 1, a building much like the one that had been the scene of the crime.

But at its door they met with a check.

'Shooting. Shooting.'

A whole little crowd blocked their way.

But the chowkidar knew the true importance of his errand.

'It is Miss Nilima who has asked the Inspector Sahib to come,' he proclaimed.

Ghote stood tall as he could and contrived an air of lofty patience while the huddle blocking his way took in the news.

'But it is Nilima they are shooting. Nilima.'

The Pathan utterly ignored this objection and in less than a minute Ghote found himself inside the building, creeping along in the dark following the chowkidar's broad back towards the set where the great Nilima was at work. It was very much reminiscent of his approach to the scene of Dhartiraj's death, except that hardly had they advanced ten yards than there was a sudden shout of 'Lights' and a blaze of whiteness struck out from some twenty or more lights high above them. It was followed at once by another shout of 'Music', a blast from a buzzer and then a blare of sound from some huge unseen loudspeakers, so noisy it immediately drowned every thought in his head.

The Pathan turned to him and leant down to whisper, though with all the noise that could hardly have been necessary.

Ghote stoically received again the blast of spiciness that told him how well the chowkidar had eaten.

'Sahib, they are picturizing on her.'

The fellow sounded as if he could not have had a bigger piece of luck than to come into the studio at this time. But what Ghote felt with fury was the familiarity with which he had used the English word 'picturizing', all the more galling because he himself was not at all sure what it meant.

But that question at least was soon to be answered. The Pathan beckoned him to follow again and in a few moments they turned a corner and were able to see the whole process going on.

In effect Nilima was being filmed, Ghote quickly realized, as if she was singing the song that, after an orchestral introduction full of the rippling of the *jal-tarang* and much swooping of many violins, the loudspeakers were now playing in the voice of a highly-skilled playback singer. Yes, he knew about those. At home whenever his son got control of the radio it was the *filmi* songs of playback singers that poured out in honeyed lilting sweetness.

Nilima was evidently taking the role of a beautiful woman trying to make up her mind what to wear for some very special occasion, perhaps her wedding, perhaps to meet the man she loved. Ghote could not decide whether the song would be part of the Macbeth story or come in some other film altogether. Certainly the setting was not a modern room and Nilima was already wearing a sari, of tremendous richness, that could have come from any time together with quantities of equally timeless

51

silver jewellery. The *almirah* too, from which she was to choose the new sari, was a large richly-carved piece that could have fitted in with almost any period of the past.

Nilima half danced, half swayed from it, her mind not at all made up, over to a huge gold-framed mirror up to which she yearningly leant, her hips moving in time to the sugary – and blaring – music.

Ghote noted that she did not look quite as magnificently beautiful seen close to as he had remembered her from the screen. It was evident, for one thing, that she was no longer in her first youth. It was evident too here that the goddess was a human being, if only because she was beginning to sweat. And certainly with the glare of the lights above them it was appallingly hot in the shut-up studio, despite the big fans that had been wheeled up to blow into the set.

'Cut! Cut! NG! NG!'

The loudspeakers whined into silence. The Pathan at his side bent his head and whispered.

'It is a No Good because of the sweat, you see, sahib.'

'Yes, yes, of course,' Ghote whispered crossly back.

A man with a make-up tray had hurried across to Nilima. Ghote wondered if his ministrations would last long enough to give himself a chance of hearing from Nilima what it was she wanted. He glanced at his watch. Time was getting on. And the fading Jagdish Rana, the only man, it seemed, with a reason to hate all-popular Dhartiraj, was still unquestioned.

But the make-up man did not take long to dab at Nilima's face with powder, spray it with rose-water, carefully wipe it dry and make some tiny final adjustments with a long brush to her eye-shadow.

'All ready?'

'Silence. *Choop chaap.* Silence.'

A hush fell.

'Lights!'

'Music!'

The buzzer blasted. The loudspeakers sprang into blaring sound.

'Camera! Action!'

52

A man with a clapper board, the Clapper Boy – Ghote knew what he was called, but only now realized that the scrawled chalk figures on the black board must indicate which scene and 'take' this was – stepped forward and clacked the board's bar down on to its base. Nilima began again her swaying, dancing progress towards the mirror.

This time no human beads of sweat interfered with the fantasy. Nilima leant yearningly into the mirror. She stepped back and turned. She began to sing.

Her voice was not beautiful, Ghote noted. But he saw that this was not at all important since she was singing only so that her lips would synchronize with the words of the playback singer. And yet . . .

Yet, even with the sweat beginning once more to penetrate the heavy layer of make up, Nilima was magical. There was no other word.

'Cut! Cut!'

Again the loudspeakers whined down to nothingness. And again the make-up man went to Nilima's assistance, not without sharp words being said about the delay his failure to deal with the perspiration problem was causing.

The delay, Ghote thought.

When would he get to Jagdish Rana at this rate? What could Nilima want with him? Would it affect the case? Was it more important than getting quickly to the fading star?

But she wanted to see him. She had sent messages specially to make sure he did not leave the Studios without coming to her. The great star.

The scene began again. And stopped, this time for some reason even the chowkidar could not understand. Then it was started once more. And stopped. And began again.

Can I believe your sugar-coated words? How many times now had he heard Nilima sing that? Always in the same slightly croaky manner?

Could such a line, sung in a song, fit somehow into the tragedy of Macbeth?

He sighed. In the film world it almost certainly could.

But suddenly loud voices were shouting and echoing 'OK'

53

'OK' and he realized that the whole business was at last over.

'Come, Inspector.'

His Pathan guide led him into the set itself and to Nilima. The fellow made her a low salaam and told her that this was the CID Inspector.

At once she took half a pace towards him and held out both her hands, palms open as if in supplication. He saw her eyes were shining with a warmth that seemed to caress him from head to foot.

'Bring chairs,' she said to the Pathan in a swift aside. 'And, Inspector, you will take something to drink? Canc-juice, Coca-Cola?'

'Yes. No. No, thank you, nothing to drink.'

He made an effort to pull himself together. It was ridiculous, really, that anyone should offer some sugary cane-juice or a cold drink in a way that sounded as if she were putting a rich pearl on a cushion of velvet before a lover. He had come to see her on a matter of business. It was possible she had information which would lead to the apprehension of a murderer. That was why he had come. Otherwise he would have been out at Juhu beach by now interrogating his most likely suspect. It was ridiculous she should make him feel like this. But she did.

'Madam,' he said, croaking out the words. 'If you are wanting to see me, I am altogether at your – Madam, I am here.'

The chowkidar returned carrying two canvas chairs, one in either hand. Ghote saw that one had printed on its back the word 'Nilima' and the other the word 'Director'. The Pathan placed Nilima's for her, his face foolishly radiant at every move. Ghote took the other chair from him and put it facing the star's.

He sat down. 'Director'.

Nilima leant forward towards him. A wave of deep and disturbing perfume reached him. He breathed in.

'Inspector,' she said, in that richly cooing voice he remembered from the darkness of all the cinemas he had seen her in. 'Inspector, I have asked you to come to make to you a plea.'

A clammy flush of sweat sprang up on the front of his thighs.

'Madam.'

He felt a tremendous urge to deliver himself of a pledge to help to his utmost, whatever request it was that she made to him. An overwhelming purposefulness seemed to emanate from the goddess sitting looking at him, not two yards away. There was something in him, deep down, that was able to attempt to analyse that purposefulness, to record coolly that it sprang no doubt from the mixture of her sheer physical perfection – even if he had noted that time had had its effects even here – combined with an uncheckable confidence in herself and in her power of securing instant attention. Yet with all his conscious mind he wanted simply to agree in advance to whatever demand she might make.

The huge almond eyes were softly beaming.

'Inspector, the death of poor Dhartiraj, it was not an accident, was it, like when that Baby fell in the studio a week or two ago and nearly killed that fellow?'

He swallowed.

'No, madam. Today's incident was in no way accidental.'

'Yes, that is what I had heard. So now I tell you, Inspector. You must solve the mystery. You must do it at once. They have been saying in the Studios that no one was seen up on the catwalk. Is that so, Inspector? Is it so?'

'Yes,' Ghote replied, his voice throbbing with emotion. 'Yes, it is so. I can tell you that.'

He had been going to add 'with all my heart' only some tiny voice inside him called up that it would be an unjustified extravagance. He contented himself instead with leaning forward as earnestly as he could.

Nilima stayed silent, as if to take his words and breathe on them the stamp of her own being.

'An invisible man,' she said at last. 'An invisible man, Inspector, and you will find him. I knew it the moment I saw you. "Here, here," I said, "is one to do it." And you can. You can. Inspector, do it. Solve this mystery.'

She moved a tiny way towards him. He felt a surge, not of desire – how could you desire a goddess? – but of willingness, of utter willingness to do anything asked of him because Nilma was asking it.

The deep-down cool voice repeated that this was only the famed aura of the film star affecting him as it had affected hundreds of thousands of others, only more closely, more intimately. But the willingness did not slacken.

'Madam, I hope – I hope to solve the myst – the matter. But let me tell you it would not be easy, not at all easy.'

Was he making it sound even harder than it was so as to please her the more? There was Jagdish Rana out at Juhu. Perhaps, had he declined to come to Nilima, he would be making the arrest even at this minute. But, no matter, if he went from her and found the murderer straightaway, what a tribute that would be to lay at her feet.

'But you would do it, Inspector.'

The pigeon-soft cloud of sound enveloped him. He felt a renewed urge to make the task sound altogether impossible.

From the pocket of his shirt he extracted – his fingers were appallingly sweat-sticky – the bundle of notes he had made during his talk with Miss Officewalla. He sorted through them scramblingly.

'Madam,' he said, as at last he found what he had been looking for, 'please to glance through the following. It is a list of those close to Mr Dhartiraj who might have had reason to want him dead. Please understand, it is not a matter of accusing any of the persons mentioned. But I wish you to see how very many people it may be necessary for me to interrogate, and even then the murderer may well not be among them.'

He thrust the list to Nilima. Their hands did not quite touch, but it seemed to him, it distinctly seemed to him, that at the tips of his fingers he had detected a tiny warmth that came from hers. There had been an exchange between them. The slightest of exchanges, but an exchange. Between Ganesh Ghote and Nilima.

But Nilima did not look at the list. Instead she held it out back to him.

'No, Inspector,' she said, the words wafted towards him. 'No, you would read it to Nilima.'

He took the sheet. He gave a small cough to clear his throat. He began to read. He stopped. His throat had remained implacably dry. He coughed again. He managed to get to the end of the list.

'Inspector, that was wonderful. Wonderful. And Nilima's name is not there.'

He felt a little shock of dismay. That Nilima should be stupid.

'But – But, madam, your name could not be on this list. It is the names only of those who had some direct link with Dhartiraj, his family, his employees, his servants, his – er – *chumchas*.'

'Inspector, you have made such a list, and so soon. Inspector, now Nilima has even more faith in you.'

She rose from her chair. There was a tinkling of silver ornaments, a stream chuckling in the hills.

Ghote, too, leapt up. The chair with the word 'Director' across its canvas back teetered dangerously. He wanted to salaam, to pour out an assurance that he would not rest till he had done what she had asked.

But some almost totally buried rational instinct told him suddenly that Nilima had not, when you thought about it, ever said to him why exactly she had asked to see him with such urgency.

'Madam,' he blurted out. 'Miss Nilima, what I am not at all understanding is why you have asked me to do this, which is after all my simple duty only?'

She turned back to him. There was a hint of disappointment on her wonderfully womanly face, the faintest pout of the lips. He felt with a jab of pain that he had failed her. He should somehow have known the answer to that question. He was not the man she had believed he was.

'That is –' he stammered. 'That is –'

A hinted smile appeared on her face, the moon almost breaking through dark clouds. It was forgiveness.

'Inspector.' Her voice conveyed that she was repeating a simple lesson to a child who had failed childishly to learn it at first telling. 'Inspector, the film. *Khoon Ka Gaddi*, the mightiest historical ever made. It stars Nilima. Inspector, the making of that film cannot be delayed.'

Chapter 7

All during the drive across to the sea at Juhu Ghote sat con-
templating his interview with Nilima, as if looking at a brightly
painted picture – or even, he thought, like a film, a film in
Technicolor.

Nilima, the great Nilima, the darling over the years of
millions, had begged him, had called to him and begged him, to
solve the mystery of the death of her fellow star. She had made
him feel he would earn her ever-present gratitude. He saw it all.
As soon as the arrest was announced she would ask him to come
to her. More. She would tell him he was welcome to visit her
whenever he wished. He would become one of her circle, her
golden circle. He would mingle with her and her fellow artistes.
The man who had solved the Dhartiraj mystery and the brilliant
stars. As one. At one.

By God, Jagdish Rana had better watch out. If the truth of it
lay there, then he would have it out of him if he had to prise it
away with his bare hands.

'Sir, this would be it.'

His driver had pulled up in front of a two-storey bungalow,
all new in shining pink paint, overlooking the wide yellowy
beach with its scatter of bathers and picnic parties, its camels
giving rides, its chiropodists and ear-cleaners and fortune-
tellers, its families of acrobats performing daring feats on their
long bamboo poles for the benefit of small circles of onlookers.

Inside the bungalow, which proved to have a huge staircase
winding up from its hallway to the modest floor above, Ghote
found that Jagdish Rana had just finished shooting his scene –
he was playing the brother of the Villain – and that there was
nothing to prevent an immediate interrogation. Except the
finding of a place to hold it. Most of the ground floor of the
house was devoted to the hallway and an enormous lounge,
complete with grand piano, where the remainder of Jagdish
Rana's scene was then being filmed. In the only other two small
rooms the owners of the house, who had, it seemed, built it for

the sole purpose of renting out to film companies, were living a cramped existence and were to be seen peering discreetly at the *filmi* goings on, two fat moony faces, one above a multi-coloured shirt, the other above a pale pink chiffon sari. Only the enormous master bedroom on the floor above appeared to be free of actors or technicians.

But it was by no means an ideal setting for a probing inter-view with a murder suspect. It was altogether too soft. It was ridiculously soft. To begin with it was carpeted, not tiled, car-peted from wall to wall in a soft creamy white such as would have shown for ever the least mark made by the accidents of everyday living. Then there were mirrors everywhere, mirrors in heavily ornate golden frames throwing back increasingly soft reflections of the whole room in endless perspectives. It was dimly lit, too, with the thick pink velvet curtains almost com-pletely drawn and lamps in pink silk shades casting soft pools of light in unnecessary places. And finally there was the bed. It was round and it was huge and it stood up on a circular platform of its own, covered by a great puffy pink circular quilt.

The quilt alone, he thought, would make even the hardest of floors more than comfortable enough to sleep on. And to sleep underneath it at any time would be an impossibility, even on those winter mornings when the water in the shower struck cold.

But the room had another enormous disadvantage as a place in which to conduct an interrogation. There was only one chair.

It was not much of a chair either, a stool-like object covered in very deeply padded pink silk standing in front of the expans-ive built-in dressing-table. But, except for the bed, it was the only thing on which to sit. He jerked it round, banged it down and lowered himself on to it, his back as straight as he could make it.

He indicated the bed to the failed star.

'Sit, Mr Rana, sit.'

Jagdish Rana stepped up on to the low platform and sank down on to the puffy pink quilt at the edge of the big round bed.

Ghote peered at him in the dim light. He very much wanted to haul back the heavy velvety curtains and let the sun flood sharply in. But to do so would alert his suspect.

Yes, despite the soft dimness, he thought he could see enough. It was plain he was facing a man on the downward slope. Under the eyes there were heavily obvious pouches. The lips below the thin line of the sharply black moustache, which he remembered now from the times he had seen this lean face painted to three or four times its true size on dozens of huge hoardings over the years, were pursed in tenseness. And no sooner had he sunk into that circular softness on the bed than the tension manifested itself.

'Inspector, I am agreeing to this interview under protest. I have already told an Assistant Inspector I saw back at Talkiestan all I know about the death of Dhartiraj. I am not to be hounded in this way.'

The pencil-thin black moustache twitched.

I have contacts in the Police Department, Inspector. I must warn you, if you detain me for one second longer than is necessary, I have telephone numbers in my little book that I can ring.'

With lean nervous fingers he tapped once sharply on what looked like a small address-book in the top pocket of his wild-silk shirt.

But Ghote, his pledge to Nilima still ringing in his head, was quick to counter this.

'Mr Rana,' he said. 'Or should I call you Mr Hari Ram?'

He saw with a stab of pride that this piece of out-of-the-way information, culled from his long session with Miss Officewalla, had paid off. Into the fading star's eyes there had come a quick look of sullen defiance. He would know now that he was not dealing with anybody who could be kept in their place by threats. It was level fighting between them, at the very least.

'Mr Hari Ram, a great star has been murdered today. Anybody who knew him and was near the scene comes under suspicion. You equally among them. Perhaps even more than equally.'

Again he saw the tired eyes flick in instant response.

'But, Inspector, why me more than others? Dhartiraj and I were the best of friends, I assure you. Co-artistes and the best of friends.'

'Yet he had shaken you from your place at the top of the tree of Villains,' Ghote replied flatly.

The thin lips tautened.

'Inspector, I am thinking you do not know so very much about the film world.'

Ghote almost leapt up and flung back at him that this was not at all the case. Was he not the chosen emissary of Nilima herself?

But he sat where he was on the softly yielding little pink stool-chair.

'Inspector,' Jagdish Rana went on, measuring him with his every word, 'Dhartiraj was a great artist. That I would be the last to deny. But there are other stars who have had success also. Perhaps from the well-known fickleness of the front-seat wallahs they have lost for a while some of their status. But they are still stars. Top stars.'

In the pinky dimness it was clear to see that suddenly control had snapped.

He leant forward from the plump bed, his tired eyes wide.

'I am one of those stars,' he went on in a voice somewhere between a snarl and a whine. 'In my day I have made *chhutti* of every other Villain actor there is, and I will again. I will. There is life enough in this body. Yes, I can act them down to the ground, I can fight with the best, I can sting.'

And he bounded to his feet, and struck a swaggering pose as if about to launch into some song that would toss verses from hero to heroine changing with each one to some new and more marvellous location, at one moment calling across from one Kashmiri peak to the next, then sweeping down a broad Bombay road sitting up on the back of an open sports car driving with two nonchalant fingers and no feet at all and then as suddenly in the romantic deserts of Rajasthan, he mounted on a white horse, she coyly amid the branches of a lone tree.

He even tossed off a few steps. Ghote waited till he had one foot high in the air and then shot in a sharp question.

'But just how long since you were in a jubilee film?'

The dance collapsed from one beat to another. Jagdish

61

Rana's face flushed a deep and ugly colour. He plunged forward towards Ghote on his little pink chair.

'Listen to me,' he yelled. 'Why do you think I told you I cannot waste time here with your ridiculous questions? Because at any minute I must go to see Seth Chagan Lal to sign for the role of Maqbet in *Khoon Ka Gaddi*. That is why.'

The moment the words were out of his mouth he must have realized what a motive for murdering Dhartiraj he had let slip. He stepped backwards away from Ghote, stumbled at the edge of the circular bed platform and almost fell.

'But – But, Inspector,' he babbled. 'But please understand. I am second to none in my admiration for Dhartiraj. Yes, he ought to have played that part. He would have been a Maqbet in a thousand. But – But the film must go on, Inspector. We are all agreed on that. Someone must play the role.'

He gave Ghote a quick little look from under his eyebrows. It reminded him of a schoolboy who had been caught out in some really serious offence, had bluffed to the hilt to get out of it and was looking up at the teacher to see if he had succeeded.

Well, he had not.

The scent of success rose suddenly in his nostrils. Perhaps the case would not after all be the long-drawn-out business he had feared. Perhaps he was going to fulfil his pledge to Nilima almost as soon as he had made it. And then . . .

For a moment he allowed a vision of himself as the affair came to its climax to hang brightly lit in his mind. The hushed court, the learned judge looking like some flapping-cheeked character actor leaning intently forward to catch the least word of the evidence, himself in the box with the spotlight playing down on – No. Not a spotlight, of course. But it would be himself in the box and he would parry with calm the last frenzied assaults of the defence pleaders. An unanswerable case. A swift and decisive verdict. And the cheers.

'Please to resume your seat, Mr Rana,' he said, chilly as water from a mountain stream.

Jagdish Rana, eyes bloodshot from the wildness of his actions, looked for one instant as if he would refuse to obey. But then he turned back to the big bed and slumped down, pushing the round feather-puffed pink quilt askew.

Drawing in a long breath, Ghote began systematically questioning him. At what time exactly had he arrived that morning at Talkiestan Studios? What had been his shooting schedule for the morning shift? Had it been kept to? What had he done while he was waiting to go before the cameras? When had he had his make-up done? How long had it taken? Who had he talked to? Who had he seen? And each answer he checked carefully against the timetable he had made out on the longest sheet of paper he had been able to find in his pockets.

Yet before long it became increasingly plain that only indefinite evidence was emerging against the fading star. True, it was possible that he could have killed Dhartiraj. During the period of only five minutes or so for which it was strictly necessary for him to have established an alibi he had not, so far as he was able to prove, been in anyone's company. Like Dhartiraj, he had been learning his dialogues, and he had retired, so he said, to his car to do so.

He made a couple of attempts to claim that he had been under observation at the time. But when Ghote telephoned Assistant Inspector Jahdev at Talkiestan both the people he had named, small-part actors, had not been prepared to say they had seen him.

On the other hand nothing emerged to disprove his contention. Assistant Inspector Jahdev put a whole squad of men on to looking for anyone who had been anywhere near the place where the Villain-player's car had been parked at the time of the murder. But he had been able to find no one definitely in the right place at the right time.

Yet motive Jagdish Rana undoubtedly had and Ghote felt loath indeed to give up the hunt. And before the interrogation was over the case against him was abruptly strengthened.

It seemed that he might too have possessed the means of committing the crime.

Assistant Inspector Jahdev had telephoned to ask for an urgent word. Ghote took the call on the extension telephone in the big bedroom, an instrument covered in its every square centimetre with tiny mosaic fragments of purple and gold Rajasthani enamel work.

He was at once assailed by a breathless account of what

someone called a setting coolie did at a film studio. It was apparently to move sets as and when required.

'A I,' he broke in eventually, 'I am quite familiar with the film world. Please go on.'

'Yes,' came his voice at last. 'Well, the thing is this. Mangu sounded very crestfallen. 'But — But, Inspector, what I was about to tell was this. You remember when I telephoned last I said that there was one fellow missing who might have been near where that car was?'

'Yes, yes.'

'Well, he was this setting coolie by the name of Mangu. And when I just now got hold of him it turned out that he was missing because he had tried to hide. He was altogether afraid, Inspector.'

'Yes, yes, man. Afraid what of?'

'That was what I was telling, Inspector. He was afraid because he had been given the job of taking back to the Property Department — you know that that is that building that is just beside the No. 2 Sound Stage, right up against the back wall of the compound, it is a long — '

'A I!'

'Yes, Inspector?'

'What was the fellow taking back there? The coolie, what's his name?'

'His name is Mangu, Inspector. Shall I spell that? It is — '

'A I, what was he taking?'

'But I was saying, Inspector, he was taking back a long, curved-blade dagger. It seems that there is a scene in this film where the Villain sees some sort of a ghost of a dagger or something of that kind. I am not — '

'Never mind the ghost. What did this Mangu tell you?'

For a long moment the line was silent while Assistant Inspector Jahdev patently tried to advance his narrative in his own mind to a point that was likely to interest the Headquarters wallah. Ghote waited with what patience he could collect. If ever this chap has to give evidence from a witness-box, he thought, he would lose his audience in no time at all.

'Yes,' came his voice at last. 'Well, the thing is this, Mangu had not taken back that dagger. He had altogether forgotten, and he remembered only when he heard about the murder. It seems that at first he thought the deed had been done with this identical weapon. But, of course it – '

'AI!'

'Yes, Inspector. Well, he found when he went to look for this dagger, which is, I am understanding, a devilishly sharp affair, he found it had been moved. To begin with he thought that somebody had – '

'AI. I do not want to know. Just tell me where the dagger is now.'

'But I was saying. It is back in Property Department. The fellow Magnu took it there as soon as he had found. It was lying – '

'He carried it to the Property Department by the handle?'

'Well, I expect so, Inspector. It would be the way that you – '

'His hands, AI? What are the condition of his hands?'

'His hands? But – I will look, Inspector. The fellow is standing right beside me now. I will look.'

It was only a few seconds later that a chastened voice said: 'They are covered in grease and dust, Inspector. It is very unlikely that there would be fingerprints, I suppose.'

Ghote banged out a few more questions to see if it had been established at just what times the dagger had been left for anyone to pick up. But the answers were unsatisfactory. The table where it had been was well out of the way. Jagdish Rana could easily have taken the weapon on his way to cut the Five-K's ropes. But so could dozens of other people.

'Thank you, AI,' Ghote said at last.

He went back to the little squabby pink chair and faced Jagdish Rana once more. He was determined not to let the least discrepancy or obscurity in anything he had said go unexamined. If there was even a hairline crack into which he could prise his way he would find it. But the interruption had not been helpful. There was a new, faintly obstinate note in the way the replies came.

And then abruptly his growing fears were realized. Jagdish Rana broke off half-way through an answer.

'Inspector,' he said, 'what is the use of you going on and on like this?'

Ghote looked at him coldly.

'I am inquiring into a case of murder,' he said. 'The murder of a great star.'

'Yes. And what have you done? Just because I have been offered the part – No, because only Seth Chagan Lal will be discussing with me whether I can play the part of Maqbet, you have got it into your head that I and I alone could have killed Dhartiraj. Well, that is ridiculous.'

Ghote, from down on his low chair, tried to hold him with his eyes.

'Mr Rana,' he said, 'you are altogether mistaken about the manner in which a murder inquiry is conducted. Let me tell you, a really experienced officer does not just pick on one suspect and try to his level best to make out a case against him. Not at all. He makes rigorous inquiries in each and every direction, and only when these are properly concluded does he make an assessment of the evidence to hand.'

'But all the same you are going on and on asking and asking me the same questions, hoping only to catch me out.'

'I am not,' Ghote shouted in fury.

But a tiny twist of knowledge inside him asserted that what the star – the falling star, curse him – was saying was true. He even had words ready in his memory to rebuke him from the great criminologist, Dr Hans Gross, whose book, edited in 1924 by J. Collyer Adam, Police Prosecutor, Madras, in its mildew-marked dark blue binding was always to hand in his office. 'The Investigator must advance step by step, making use only of such definite opinions as may be prudently formed from events as they arise.' But, fired by Nilima's appeal, he had plunged like a madman at the first indication of a possible lead.

Yet, even now, he fought to suppress that wriggle of disquiet.

'Mr Rana,' he said, 'it is up to you to realize that you are in a very serious position. You yourself have admitted to me that you had the very strongest motive for wishing Dhartiraj dead. You have no alibi at all for the time in question. And, let me tell you, the knife which was almost certainly used to cut the ropes of that Five-K, was easily available to you. It is altogether a damn poor outlook for you.'

'But, Inspector, I am not the only one with a motive.'

'No? No? Well, what others are there?' Ghote raged.

He ferreted out furiously the list he had made with the help of Miss Officewalla. It was looking more than a little battered now and he hated its creases and crossings-out.

And Jagdish Rana, he saw, was leaning back on the bed now, pillowing his head on the heaped mound of the puffy quilt, his legs dangling idly.

'If I must teach you your job, Inspector,' he drawled.

'Teach – '

Ghote spluttered. He knew that he was spluttering. His vision of himself going to Nilima before the sun had set on Dhartiraj's killing and telling her that the mystery of her fellow star's death had been solved was fast vanishing. And its going was bitter.

'Yes, Inspector,' Jagdish Rana said, all the more effortlessly cool for his own rage. 'There is certainly one other person who has a motive that is a great deal stronger than the heap of nonsense you have tried to put on to me.'

'And who is that? Who? Who?'

Jagdish Rana allowed himself the luxury of a slow smile. It was the smile he must have used in countless films playing a Villian outsmarting the Hero in the early part. And Ghote, from his faint memories of posters and hoardings, knew it. It was gall to see.

'Who are you trying to name?' he shouted. 'I must warn you that –'

'Inspector, have you considered the fellow, Sudhaker Wani?'

'Sudhaker Wani? Who the – Well, yes, naturally, he is one of the names . . .'

He rapidly spread out his tattered list on his knee, though he well knew that this was not a name Miss Officewalla had even mentioned. Yet it was vaguely familiar. He tried hard to think where he had heard it recently.

Jagdish Rana lounged back against the quilt, one eyebrow raised.

Was it the name of some star? Would a star's name be so

utterly unknown to him? He brought himself to acknowledge that it might. But if the name Sudhaker Wani – it certainly hardly sounded like that of a star – was one he ought to have recognized and had not, then . . . Then the only thing to do was to admit his ignorance and ask.

He cleared his throat.

'Please be so good as to tell me about him,' he said.

And he pulled a fresh sheet of paper out of his pocket and poised his ballpoint.

'Sudhaker Wani, as you know,' Jagdish Rana said with a thin smile, 'is a stand-in at Talkiestan. Today he was working for Dhartiraj even. But he is also more than a stand-in.'

Ghote remembered at once where he had heard the name. Sudhaker Wani was the person who had nearly been killed when that Lights Boy had let the Baby fall. He had even seen him, dressed in a *filmi* rich rajah robe, when he had first gone to the scene of the crime.

'Yes?' he said.

'Inspector,' Jagdish Rana said, stepping from word to word, 'have you ever come across fellows who, though they are in some fifth-class position only, occupy much higher places in reality? Sometimes they are big union-wallahs holding down no more than a peon's job. Or it may be a man who works as a clerk in some office but who is also a pandit to whom everybody goes for advice.'

'Yes?'

'Well, Sudhaker Wani is such a man. He is not a pandit, far from it. Prayers and advice are not at all his line. Or not the sort of advice a pandit would give. Because Sudhaker Wani will give advice all right on such matters as erotic powders and charms against this and charms against that. He has an old aunt only who makes such things, and, believe me, he is very popular around the Studios on account of her.'

He came to a halt.

'Go on,' Ghote said.

'Inspector,' the fading star continued, almost wheedlingly, 'there are other things also that man does. If, for instance, anybody is wanting to go to a blue film show somewhere around

Colaba or in some empty flat in Pedder Road, it is to Sudhaker Wani they go to ask where they can find.'

'Well?'

Jagdish Rana smiled very slightly.

'Well, tell me, Inspector, why should Dhartiraj be having a secret conversation with such a man as that?'

He let the question hang in the air.

'If Dhartiraj should have wanted some of these erotic powders,' Ghote suggested at last.

'Pah. A man like Dhartiraj to go to a hole-and-corner fellow like him. No, Inspector, if Dhartiraj was wanting such things he would pay one thousand rupees or more and go to a genuine sexology specialist. Doesn't he throw Rupees 125 per peg to drink Royal Salute whisky? Isn't that a well-known fact?'

It was not to Ghote.

'Yes, yes,' he agreed. 'That is well-known.'

'Well then, why should Dhartiraj be talking to such a fellow?' Jagdish Rana leant sharply forward. 'I will answer that in one, Inspector. The fellow must have believed he had a hold over Dhartiraj. It has been said often enough that if you buy from that old auntie of his, you pay twice. Once for what you get, once to keep his silence. Well, he is just the sort of fellow to have found out some secret of Dhartiraj's. And then he would try to get money out of him. Isn't it? Isn't it?'

The fading star was leaning well forward now, his feet planted on the creamy carpet of the round bed platform, his body tense and urgent.

'But Dhartiraj was not at all the sort of chap you could do that to,' he went on. 'He would laugh only. Or more likely, much more likely, he would tell the fellow straight out "It is the police for you, bhai" or "It is straight to Production Manager I am going, and out of the Studios for you altogether." That was the sort of fellow Dhartiraj was.'

Jagdish Rana leant another inch forward. The very pouches under his eyes seemed to have been pulled away to nothingness from the intensity of his effort.

'Well, Inspector, what is Sudhaker Wani to do now? He is threatened in every direction. He will be turned out of the

Studios where he is making so much money, and every anna of it in black. Or he will be handed over to the police. He is a desperate man.'

'Go on,' Ghote said.

'It is simple, Inspector. Today he comes to take his place as Dhartiraj's stand-in. He is sent away to get more jewels for the turban. And, just as he goes, he sees that Five-K hanging in the darkness over the man's head like a sword only. He snatches up that dagger. He runs up the ladder. Cut, cut. He slices through the ropes. The Five-K falls. He is saved.'

And he gave a mighty kick as he brought the accusation to a finish.

The giant round bed, to his utter surprise and even more to Ghote's, shot away on its central pivot and spun round and round in a mad whirl of triumph.

Chapter 8

The cry came high in the sun-baked air, just beginning to lose its hard brightness with the onset of evening, as Ghote, the urgency of his mission sprawling over his mind, hurried from his car parked just off the rutted and dusty road towards the silhouetted outline of the old ruinous building.

'Pack up. Pack up.'

He almost broke into a run.

Was he going to be too late? Would his man have finished his work and have gone off by the time he reached the Haunted Palace? And was that really, really, what the place was called?

Striding over the tussocky brown-dried grass of the uneven ground rising up from the tranquil tree-fringed expanse of Lake Powai – seemingly a totally country scene, though the huge belching mills of North Bombay lay not so far away – he strove to remember exactly what had been said to him at the Talkiestan Studios when he had raced back there from his interview with Jagdish Rana at Juhu. It had taken infuriatingly long to track down anybody at the Studios who could tell him anything about Sudhaker Wani, stand-in and go-between, even simply where he was to be found. Often enough, though, a certain evasiveness had made it clear that many people in the Studios knew the stand-in all too well.

It was from the Production Manager's secretary, a big blowsy Goan girl, whom he had first passed over in favour of going straight to her boss at the top, that he eventually got his answer.

'That man.'

There had been stormy washes of emotion in the way she had spoken of him. Of fear. Or revulsion.

He had wondered briefly whether there might not have been a history of something like an abortion, performed, in disgusting conditions, by the fellow's aunt. But he had such much more important matters to deal with.

'That man. He is at Haunted Palace this shift. Sethji has said that shooting on *Khoon Ka Gaddi* must not be halted. So they are carrying on out there with the scene where the banana grove comes to Dehra Dun.'

But was it really called the Haunted Palace, this ruin of a building gradually emerging as he hurried forward through a screen of low heat-stunted trees? He did not want to make a mistake, if the name was only one of those *filmi* jokes. Miss Officewalla had said that film people spent much of their time joking. But it would not at all do for the investigator of the murder of Dhartiraj to look a fool.

He hurried through the trees, and the ruin stood plainly before him, a substantial building which well might once have been a nawab's palace endowed with a peaceful lake view. On the smooth grass of what must once have been a garden there was a group of twenty or thirty people standing idle. Some he recognized. There beside his camera was the Cameraman – No, Director of Photography – and those must be his assistants beside him. And there was the Audiographer fellow. And now emerging from the ruined house, there was Director Bhabani Ghosh, swaying-bellied in his flowing white muslin kurta. And it was plain that most of the others standing about among the tall reflector screens on their long thin black legs were actors or extras, busy disrobing themselves of the costumes of foot-soldiers from some historical time. And there were coolies too and, sitting on the ground with a pack of cards, technicians of some sort. On the fringe there was the usual collection of urchins. Some were trailing dusty and broken blade-shaped banana leaves.

Yes, 'till Birnam Wood do come to Dunsinane'. But where was Maqbet? Where was Dhartiraj's stand-in? Dhartiraj's murderer perhaps?

He scanned the group almost frantically for the somewhat hang-dog figure he remembered all too vaguely from the circle of people standing round the body of Dhartiraj. No. No one he could recall.

Had that Goan girl, the Production Manager's secretary, been lying? Was that why she had seemed disturbed?

He broke into a run and thrust himself without ceremony between Director Ghosh and the Cameraman who had just embarked on an earnest conversation.

'Sudhaker Wani,' he burst out, 'Sudhaker Wani, the stand-in? He has been here? He is here somewhere now? I demand to see him.'

The big Bengali director stepped back a pace.

'Why, it is the Inspector,' he said, 'Inspector Ghote, isn't it?'

'Yes, yes. But Sudhaker Wani, where is he?'

Bhabani Ghosh's bold-featured face broke into a wide, easy smile.

'But, Inspector, he is right beside us. Here. This is him.'

He gestured towards the two men Ghote had taken for the Cameraman's assistants. And it was true. The one on the left was surely the fellow he had seen in the morning. Then he had been wearing, rather sheepishly, a rich red rajah's robe and now, whatever costume he had had for the shooting taken off, he was dressed just in a pair of dirtyish khaki trousers and a dull blue shirt on which at some time a right-angled tear had been mended not very skilfully. But it was the same man.

Ghote stopped to take a long hard look at his face. It was not one that would ever be easy to remember. The trick was to seize on the most notable feature and let it soak into the mind while repeating as many times as possible the name. But Sudhaker Wani — Sudhaker Wani, Sudhaker Wani, Sudhaker Wani — did not seem to have any one single really distinguishing mark. Mouth, ears, chin, eyebrows were all smallish and totally regular, seeming to retreat into the neither light nor dark flesh. His body, too, was as average as could be, neither fat nor thin, not tall nor short. Ordinary.

And the fellow's eyes, when he at last addressed him, hardly moved up at all to look at him.

'Sudhaker Wani, I am an officer of Crime Branch CID investigating the death of Dhartiraj and I wish to ask you a number of questions.'

'Very good.'

It was a low, characterless murmur.

Excusing himself to Director Ghosh, Ghote took a quick look round and decided that as good a place as anywhere to conduct the interview would be the interior of the Haunted Palace.

Inside the ruin, an empty shell, its floor strewn with brick dust and fragments of white stone, the trapped air noticeably muggier than the now cooling out-of-doors and smelling acridly of bird lime, there seemed to be only one room that was almost intact, though it too was open to the faintly darkening sky. Ghote led the way into it and took as a seat the ledge of the single tall frameless window.

Sudhaker Wani stood in front of him, waiting impassively.

He had intended to begin by asking him directly exactly what he had been doing during the few minutes when Dhartiraj had been alone on the *gaddi* learning his dialogues. Jagdish Rana's vivid account of how the fellow must have seen the poised Five-K as he had gone to take away the turban to be more ornately jewelled, of how he had snatched up the waiting dagger, of how he had climbed the ladder in the darkness, had slipped along the catwalk and had sliced through the ropes in two quick cuts, was so clear in his mind that he had thought he would not have been able to wait one instant before testing its reality. But, cooled perhaps by his ridiculous mistake in not at once recognizing the man he had pursued so hotly, he sat for some while just looking at him, and when he did put a question it was one that was almost totally irrelevant.

'Tell me, when you wear those rich clothes with all the jewels on them, what do you feel?'

But even the oddity of the question was powerless to affect the immobile figure standing in front of him.

'Inspector, I do not mind,' he answered, without a single flicker of those steadily downward-held eyes.

'No,' Ghote said, 'I am not asking if you mind. I am asking: does it make you feel different, to be dressed as a rajah?'

'No, Inspector.'

Again there was not a flicker of interest in the answer, not even the tiniest hint of surprise.

'But, look, I am asking out of interest only,' Ghote persisted. 'I have not seen very much of filming, and I wondered what it does to people to wear the clothes of someone else. It is something that affects me, you know. When I have to wear uniform I feel altogether different from myself in shirt and pants only. Do you follow that?'

'Yes, Inspector.'

But he might equally well have said 'No'.

'And you tell me,' Ghote said, with a spurt of exasperation, 'that to wear the clothes of a rich and powerful man does not at all put it into your head what it must be like to be such a one, to order men about, to turn them out of their homes, to put them to death even?'

Just for an instant then the downward-held eyes did flicker. But it was so little that he doubted what he had seen.

'Inspector,' the fellow answered in the same uninflected voice in which he had replied to every question, 'I am stand-in only.'

'But you are not stand-in only.'

The fellow had given him an opening and he seized on it. Was it the first step of a path that would lead to heights which only a few hours ago, at the start of this extraordinary day, had been utterly inconceivable?

'Inspector?'

'You are not stand-in only, Sudhaker. You also perform many different services for people in the Studios, isn't it?'

'Inspector?'

'Do not pretend with me. I know already a great deal about you. You have an aunt, isn't it? An aunt who makes mixtures of herbs and secret ingredients which people buy for large sums? Is it from her that the stars get their bed-smasher *paans* which to chew only is said to increase the potency like a bull's? Those and other things? Is it? Is it?'

'Inspector, I do have auntie.'

'And through you she sells such things.'

He hammered it at him.

'Inspector, there is no harm. The things they buy do not truly harm those they are given to. Maybe they are sometimes making a girl thin or some such thing. But, Inspector, in the West many girls are wanting all the time to slim.'

Ghote trod down this hint of rebellion as if he was squashing an unpleasant insect.

'Listen to me, Sudhaker. In Vigilance Branch they are keeping a file on you only. You are damn lucky not to be in the lock-up already.'

At last there was a clear reaction in those downward-looking eyes. A side-glancing flick of fear.

'Now, the blue films,' Ghote plunged in, feeling coiling up inside him the possibility of complete success and the heady scent of all that it could lead to.

His ferocity with the one hint of knowledge he had about the fellow's activities seemed to pay off. Though information came in driblets, it came. It was necessary whenever there was a pause only to tap impatiently with his foot on the fragments of brick and stone on the floor to get the flow to start again.

There was, it came out, not only the sessions of blue-film viewing for which the stand-in acted as organizer, but he was also involved in their making. He found technicians who would be willing to shoot them at an out-of-the-way bungalow at Dahisar and he found girls and men from among the Decent Extras willing to act in them. He even contacted smugglers to take the finished prints by sea to the Arab countries where they were especially popular.

'No, no, Inspector, I am telling you. The films we are showing in Bombay are different. They are from Sweden-Denmark. The girls we are having to use to make here are mostly too thin. Only the Arabs are liking.'

At this new sign of returning confidence Ghote tapped his foot with more than usual sharpness. Let the fellow understand he was not dealing with anyone who could be trifled with.

'Inspector,' the stand-in promptly admitted, 'it is because there is too much risk. If they seized any films in Vigilance, they could recognize the girls and lead from them to everybody.'

'And the girls?' Ghote asked, taking a small chance so as to keep his ever-speeding initiative. 'You make use of them in other ways for people who can pay?'

'There is that demand also, Inspector.'

Another quick tap of the foot.

'Rupees 500, Inspector.'

Tap, tap.

'Sometimes Rupees 1000. But that is lucky. I am not making so much, Inspector. There are many, many expenses.'

'But no tax returns. Every anna of it in black for you, Sudhaker.'

He felt a spasm of anger zig-zag through his head. The claims the tax man made on his own limited pay and the slow way in which Dearness Allowance was screwed up rupee by rupee against the ever-leaping cost of living. But he brought himself under control. Only clear thinking would keep this flow of answers running.

'But the girls are not all,' he said levelly, certain from the mere attitude of the man in front of him that the well had yet to be emptied.

'Yes, I am getting people things also. Things that are hard to get.'

Smuggling. Of course he would be a distributor of smuggled goods as well as concerned with taking blue films out.

'What things, Sudhaker?'

Get as many details as possible, get him to feel he was in it so deep he could only keep on telling the truth.

'Inspector, you know what it is film people are always want-

76

ing. It is big foreign television sets now, and watches with digital face.'

Digital face? Oh yes, no hands but little numbers instead.

He tapped his foot once more.

'But, Inspector, when they can afford and afford. To a star what is a thousand bucks even? It is nothing, less than nothing.'

This is it, Ghote thought. Now is my chance. Push on to the heart of it now.

For a moment he almost saw a glittering panorama spread out in front of his eyes.

But in fact in the little room the light had become plainly bad. Above the roofless ruin the sky was now a dark blue, the colour it would hold for only a few minutes before darkness swept over it.

Nothing for it, however, but to seize the opportunity.

'Yes,' he said. 'A thousand rupees is less than nothing to a star, especially a star like Dhartiraj.'

He leant forward sharply in the failing light to catch the least change of expression on the stand-in's impassive face. But there seemed to be nothing. And nor were there signs more tell-tale, any alterations in the way the hands were held, or the weight on the feet distributed or in the posture of the body.

But he had not answered.

'Well?'

'Dhartiraj?' the stand-in repeated tonelessly. 'Yes, I suppose he could pay better than anyone else, except Ravi Kumar.'

For a moment Ghote was tempted to pursue this fleeting mention of the superstar who had, after all, a strong motive for killing his rival in love. But he had not been in the Studios when the murder had taken place and he must therefore be left out of account. Nor must this fellow be left for one instant off the hook.

'You suppose that Dhartiraj would pay well,' he said, jabbing the words out. 'Then, tell me, what did he pay? What did he pay you for?'

'Inspector, nothing.'

'I know better than that. You have been seen talking to

Dhartiraj when no one was near. Why would he talk to you unless it was to buy?'

It was taking another chance, to presume so much from something Jagdish Rana had said almost in passing. But the guesses he had made up till now had paid off handsomely.

'Well?'

'Inspector, no.'

Yet the fellow did not seem to be denying it with much emotion. And he must have realized that the question was leading to an accusation that he had killed the star.

'Do not lie to me, Sudhaker. You were seen, I tell you.'

'Inspector, no. Dhartiraj was not the sort of man who buys from Durga Auntie. A man like him would never want anything to harm – would never want a love potion, Inspector. And if he wanted, he would go to a big sexologist fellow. He had that much money.'

Ghote saw the force of that. But he was determined not to be checked.

'Yes,' he said, 'Dhartiraj was rich. But he cannot always have been so. He rose to fame. So, when he was not so rich, what was it that he bought from you?'

It was almost dark in the little ceilingless room now. Inwardly Ghote cursed.

'Well? Answer. Answer.'

'Inspector, nothing. I have said.'

'Not things to harm perhaps. He was not the sort of person to want to harm. But something to be ashamed. Did he buy that, Sudhaker?'

'No, Inspector.'

'Something not at all harmful in itself, but something that now he would not like the *filmi* magazines to know about and to print? Yes, Sudhaker? Yes?'

Still the fellow stood there impassively in front of him. But surely he must realize that the question hit at him deeply.

It was almost impossible to see his face any longer. Ghote realized that at the back of his mind he had been aware that the sounds of the film crew departing had ceased some time before. The last car had gone revving and bucketing along the unmade-up track back to the road.

'Sudhaker Wani, when you were told by Dhartiraj this morning to take Maqbet's turban and get more jewels put on it, what did you do?'

'Inspector, I took it to Property Department.'

'Straightaway, Sudhaker?

'Yes, Inspector, straightaway.'

Ghote strove to analyse the totally placid tone of the fellow's reply. It surely could not have meant that he had indeed gone straight to the Property Department and talked with someone there the whole time that the murder had been done. Then there would surely have been a tinge of boasting in it. And, if he believed that he had succeeded in setting up a false alibi, there would have been a trace of defiance. Or, if the reply had been merely the best he could think up, there could not then but have been a hint of tenseness.

And there had been none of those things. Just a seemingly blank indifference. As if there was something altogether more important to the fellow than his questions. And that could not be. What was the fellow, after all? A stand-in only, a man in a job that required only the endurance to stand where he was put for long-long periods. All right, he had his other activities too. But, though no doubt they brought him a good deal of money, there could be nothing in his life that could make him careless of the threat of a murder charge.

Yet he seemed totally unaffected.

A streak of despair shot through his head. Why was he faced with this? He ought at this instant to have been beginning to get from this sullen figure a confession to murder. A confession to murdering Dhartiraj, the star. The first steps on an ever-widening path that would have brought him to that almost unimaginable moment of dazzle-lit recognition.

With heavy weariness he put the next question.

'You say you went straight to the Property Department with that turban. Is there anybody who could swear to that?'

'Inspector, I was there.'

'But who will swear to it?'

'There must be many people, Inspector.'

Must there? Not if the fellow had not been there at all.

'Who, Sudhaker, who?'

'Inspector, there will be many people.'

He pushed himself to his feet.

'That we would see,' he said.

Chapter 9

It did not take long to get Sudhaker Wani put in the lock-up at the police-station nearest to Talkiestan Studios under Assistant Inspector Jahdev's charge. Ghote felt happier when it was done. With every passing minute he was beginning to feel more and more sure that the charge that would eventually be brought would come under Section 201 of the Indian Penal Code: murder.

Nothing the fellow had given away so far could lead to the charge, though there were things that needed explanation – if only his comparative willingness to talk about his smuggling and offences against Section 292 (Obscene books and films) compared with his later blank indifference. But no doubt some sort of answer to that would emerge. And perhaps the contrast just did not matter. If he could be shown to have been lying about what he was doing at the time Dhartiraj had been killed, then the whole situation would look different.

'Get a move on,' he snapped at his driver, who was finding it hard to work his way through the last of the evening traffic rush.

The man glanced round to him as if surprised at his impatience.

He glared straight ahead, determined to offer no explanation.

Get to the Studios, get over to the Property Department, pin down whoever was there. And then, if it emerged that Sudhaker had been lying . . . Then tear the fellow apart. Get him down to Headquarters and make him talk if it took all night. Because what a morning it would be after. The dawning of what a day. The beginning of an altogether new life.

But at the Studios gate he met a check.

As his car approached, two chowkidars – different men from

the ones he had seen before – came running out into the road-way, holding up their hands to stop the traffic. One came right up and stood there bang in front of his vehicle.

A flare of rage ripped across his mind. What the hell was the man up to? What did he mean stopping him like this?

But a moment later he saw what it was all about.

From out of the widely opened gates there slid, smooth as a python, a huge limousine. And, seated at the back, all alone and looking like a maharajah in his durbar hall, there was Seth Chagan Lal.

If anything Ghote's rage fanned up yet higher.

Oh yes, Seth Chagan Lal was a Producer, a man who held even the fortunes of stars in his hand. But what right had he to take priority over an investigation into the murder of a man who was the idol of millions? He had half a mind –

But already the long limousine was gliding round his own battered vehicle. He slumped back in his seat.

And then, with a bouncing jerk, the limousine came to a halt exactly parallel with him. He saw the Seth jabbing crossly at some buttons. He must at last have hit the right one because the window directly between them slipped suddenly smoothly down and a waft of air-conditioned coolness reached out to him on his hot leather seat.

'Ah, Inspector, it is good I have seen.'

'Yes, Mr Lal? Yes, sir?'

He wished he had not sounded so much like a clerk, or a servant even.

'What so far have you found out?'

He hesitated. Should he tell him that what he had found out was a police matter and that no one, whoever they might be, had any right to know?

The tight blubber face was looking at him with unwavering intensity, eyes stonelike, slit mouth closed. It was no more than two feet away.

Well, there were people who, if they asked a question like that even out of casual interest only, you gave some sort of full answer to. Influential people. People you wanted to have on your side, the police side.

'Sir, we are making progress.'

'Progress, progress. Inspector, I have publicity managers one, two, three, to tell people things like that. But I am asking you what has happened in the case. Seth Chagan Lal is asking, Inspector.'

'Sir, we have pursued several lines of inquiry.'

A glint of anger showed in the little stone eyes.

Ghote swallowed.

'And – And already I have one of the Studios' employees behind the bars.'

There was a moment's silence. Then the hard voice came again.

'But you are not charging him with the murder of Dhartiraj.'

'Yes. Yes, that is true. Most sagacious of you, Sethji. It is an employee whose other offences have come to light.'

Why did he do it? 'Most sagacious of you, Sethji.' And he was meant to be the star investigator, the match of any man.

'But why is the fellow not charged with murder? Why, Inspector?'

'Sir – Sethji, we are not having adequate evidence.'

'Evidence, evidence. You have got there behind the bars a criminal, isn't it? You have found a criminal in the Studios. Well, then, it is likely-likely, I am telling you, that he can be found guilty of the murder. Charge him, Inspector, charge.'

'No, sir.'

He drew himself up straight on the scuffed leather of the car seat.

'Inspector, what are you meaning "No"? I am saying, Inspector, that it is altogether best if someone is charged. The murder of Dhartiraj is a damn serious matter, Inspector. Serious for Talkiestan Studios, serious for Fifteen Arts Films. You have got a man there. Charge him.'

'Mr Lal, not only is there no firm evidence against him but it is possible he may prove to have a good alibi. No question of a charge can arise.'

'No, Inspector? Perhaps we would have to see.'

The blubber face was hard as tyre-rubber.

Ghote found himself, almost without realizing what he was

doing, making a peace offering. After all, Sudhaker Wani was not the only man he had under suspicion. If the case against the stand-in did after all fall down when he came to make his inquiries, then there was still something that Jagdish Rana would have to answer.

'On the other hand, Mr Lal, there is the possibility of a case against another individual. I am talking in strictest confidence, please understand.'

'Inspector, when you are talking to Seth Chagan Lal you are talking at VIP level. Always.'

'Yes, sir. Of course, sir.'

'Then who is this man?'

Damn. Damn. Damn.

He had not intended to name a name. He had succeeded after all in keeping Sudhaker Wani's actual name out of it. But now, thanks to trying to butter Seth Chagan Lal with talk about 'strictest confidence', he had got himself faced with the direct question. Was there no way out?

None showed itself.

'Sir, it is – It is a star that I am having to name, sir.'

The blubber face, so close to his own, darkened in an instant with massive emotion. The stone eyes glared like twin sports-car headlamps set beside the everyday orangey glow of Ambassadors and Fiats.

Of course, film stars were the Seth's great stock in trade. To lose one would be like a diamond merchant in the Zaveri Bazaar losing one of his precious gems. But such searing rage as this . . .

'Who is it, Inspector? Who?'

The voice compelled with all the willpower that had taken the man from a scraping clerk's existence to his present riches and esteem.

'Sir, it is Jagdish Rana.'

The Seth's face changed in an instant.

'Jagdish Rana,' he exclaimed, his voice crackling now with mere exasperation. 'You were talking of stars.'

Ghote felt sharply offended. Once again his assessment of some aspect of the *filmi duniya* was being scorned. But Jagdish

Rana was a star, however firmly on the downward path. He was. Not only had he claimed it himself with much drama, but *filmi* people still called him a star. Miss Officewalla even had done so. It was unfair.

'But sir,' he burst out, 'you yourself are even considering him for the role of Maqbet in *Khoon Ka Gaddi*.'

And then the hard blubber face split open in brief laughter.

'Jagdish Rana, Maqbet. Maqbet, Jagdish Rana. Oh Inspector, Inspector, you have no idea. You are having no idea at all. Arrest Jagdish Rana if you like. Arrest him three-four times and there is nothing to care. Nothing at all to care.'

The big air-conditioned limousine had shot off into the darkness, leaving Ghote with one final glimpse of the Seth pushing and jabbing happily at his buttons to get the window to go up. He himself had not ordered his driver to go on into the Studios. Instead he had sat there letting the traffic whir by and had thought.

There was a lot to think about.

First, there was the fact that Seth Chagan Lal's derisive permission to him to arrest Jagdish Rana had precisely cleared the failing star. If there was no chance at all of the fellow stepping into Dhartiraj's shoes in the part of Maqbet, then he hardly had a motive for wanting to get Dhartiraj out of the way. What the fellow had said to him out at Juhu had been only the wildest of boasting.

So, if when he made his inquiries at the Property Department here he found that Sudhaker Wani's offered alibi did in fact stand up, then he would have no real line to pursue. So that alibi must be false. He must get his hands on Dhartiraj's murderer. He must. That was what it was all about. The vision.

'Go in, man,' he snapped at the driver. 'What for are you sitting about here all night? Go in.'

But as the car went on up to the Studios gates something else that he knew he ought to think about emerged like an iron rock in his head. It was Seth Chagan Lal's whole attitude. It was not somehow what it ought to be. It had been much too concerned all along, both just now and this morning.

Yet why that should be defied guessing. And they were through the gates now and making their way through splashy pools of light to the Property Department.

Well, there his answer would lie. Must lie. Sudhaker Wani's alibi must be broken.

Only at the Property Department he found that he had forgotten in his absorption in the importance of the case one simple thing. That ordinary people had ordinary lives to live. None of the staff in the Property Department were the same as those who had been there first thing in the morning.

He stood feeling foolish. Damn it, he ought to have realized when he had seen that different chowkidars were on duty at the gates. A film studio, working three shifts a day, could not have the same personnel there from start to finish.

For a few moments he planned furiously how he could get a list of the home addresses of everyone who had been on duty in the Property Department that morning from Manager to humblest coolie, how he would go all over Bombay finding them one by one, dragging what he wanted to know out of them.

But before very long he realized that even a whole night would not be time enough for that. And – he asked and they confirmed it for him – before eight o'clock next morning every one of the people he wanted to see would be back in the Studios.

Slowly a cold greyness rose up in him, blotting out the fiery ambition that had lasted in him ever since he had had that interview with Sudhaker Wani and before. No, there was one way to conduct an inquiry and one way only. And that was systematically to interview everybody who might have any light to throw on the circumstances, whether they seemed likely suspects or not.

He had people he ought to be interviewing on these lines. The names on the list he had compiled with Miss Officewalla's help. None of them was a very likely murderer of the dead star. Miss Officewalla had made that quite clear. But in logic they might have killed him, and it was his duty to check on their whereabouts at the time of the crime. If it took him all night.

It did take him most of the night.

Dhartiraj's personal astrologer – that saintly old man – proved to be much concerned to explain how the star's horoscope had accurately predicted that this was a most inauspicious period for him, and had incidentally mentioned that he had been conferring with fellow pandits at the time Dhartiraj had died. The dead star's former wife, now the embittered Mrs Ravi Kumar, had taken a long while to track down but then had said convincingly that she had not seen Dhartiraj for many months and that she had been under the hands of her hairdresser at the time he had died. The as yet unfilmed new star, Meena, Dhartiraj's keep, looking every bit as thin as Miss Officewalla had said she would, had been in floods of tears. But eventually she had remembered that she had been in bed that morning till very late and there were two of her servants to prove it. He had questioned them thoroughly, just as he had questioned Mrs Kumar's hairdresser and, just as with him, he had eventually satisfied himself that what he had been told was true.

Dhartiraj's make-up man had been, he claimed, in vigorous dispute with Nilima's make-up man at the time of the death on the relative merits of home-produced and foreign-smuggled cosmetics. And Nilima's make-up man, who lived in a particularly crowded area in Dadar and who had not at all liked being woken in the middle of the night, had eventually agreed that this had been so. Dhartiraj's secretary had been busy with the star's mail at the time of his death, and luckily had had to consult his Personal Assistant over much of it. So eliminating them had not taken as long as it might have done.

But it was in the very early hours of the morning that Ghote managed to get home at last for an hour or two's sleep. And he had done so with the additional depressing knowledge that none of the people he had spoken to had been able to suggest anyone who had even remotely disliked the ever-popular player of Villains enough to have wanted to kill him for any reason whatsoever.

When the alarm clock on the little shelf above the bed clangingly woke him next day his mood had not changed. He saw only a long slog before him. Even the prospect of being able within an hour or so to check Sudhaker Wani's alibi with the people who had been in the Property Department the previous morning did not fill him with yesterday's enthusiasm.

Thank goodness, he thought, that I missed the Press last evening. If I had told them that someone had been 'helping with inquiries', what would they have expected? A brilliant solution to the killing of a brilliant figure?

He arrived at the Studios as early as any of the employees, and tackled the business of checking on Sudhaker Wani's presence in the Property Department filled with a premonition that he was going to find that the stand-in had at least a reasonable alibi.

And if that proved so, he thought, it would be the painful round of examining every less and less likely possibility until in the end there was none left and other routine tasks would assert their claims even over the case of the murdered film star.

But, quite soon, he found that the stand-in hardly had an alibi at all.

True, he had brought the Maqbet turban to the Property Department and had handed it over with Dhartiraj's instructions. But as soon as he had done so he had left.

'Where did he go? Did you see? Where?' he asked the Department Manager, who had taken charge of the turban himself.

'Inspector, he might have gone to a hundred and one places. He might have wanted a *bidi* only, and smoking is strictly forbidden within the walls of my department.'

'But Sudhaker Wani did not smoke,' the Department Sub-Manager, hovering helpfully, put in.

His superior rounded on him at once.

'I dare say, I dare say, Sub-Manager. But a man has many other reasons for not wanting to stay. There is always the call of nature, you know.'

'Yes, Manager sahib,' the Sub-Manager dutifully replied.

But, as Ghote left, he heard him mutter, 'But I think Sudhaker did not have those even.'

He wondered briefly at the words. They confirmed his own

feelings about the stand-in as a man somehow different from the human majority. But the thought faded.

What was important was that, once more, he had a strong suspect. Sudhaker Wani had not stayed inside the Property Department, as he had implied the evening before. He had lied about that. And if he had not stayed there, there was plenty of time for him to have hurried back to Sound Stage No. 2 – it was only a few yards – to have quietly taken the curved dagger from its table, to have slipped across to the ladder up to the catwalk, to have made his way swiftly to the dangling Five-K, to have slashed – once, twice – at its ropes, and easily in the ensuing confusion to have got back to the Property Department, replacing the dagger more or less in its original position on the way.

He could have done it all. He must have done it. He must be made to confess that he had done it. It was still less than twenty-four hours since the crime had been committed. To have solved the mystery in that time. It would be a star performance. A true star performance.

Chapter 10

Sitting fuming with impatience in his Headquarters office, Ghote saw with pouncing pleasure, when at last a couple of Assistant Inspector Jahdev's constables brought Sudhaker Wani in, that he was looking a good deal worse for his night in the lock-up. A spell in such a place, narrow, high-walled, probably no bigger in area than the veranda outside, ventilated only by its tall barred gate, pungent with the combined stink of as many as a hundred prisoners stripped to undershorts and sandals, was a pretty good way of splintering almost any shell of pride.

Had it then been only pride that had sustained the fellow during his previous interrogation? Would it be no more now than a question of using rather tougher methods than he had employed the day before? It certainly looked, if only just, as if the fellow was not after all so hardened against attack as he had seemed.

So, be that little more tough and perhaps before even half an hour was up the confession would be pouring out, the first step on the upward rising path to such blazing heights it was not possible to think about.

'So, Sudhaker, last night you told me that you went from Dhartiraj to the Property Department and that there were plenty of people who saw you there. Suppose that now you give me their names.'

'Inspector, I cannot.'

Those eyes were fixed, obstinately as ever, on a spot just a foot or so below his own.

'You cannot, Sudhaker?' He put a plainly jeering note into his voice. 'You cannot? Not one only even? Not one person who saw you in the Property Department?'

'Inspector, I gave the turban to Manager sahib. Sub-Manager sahib was there also.'

'Yes, you gave. And then you went straight out.'

Silence.

'Well yes or no? You went out?'

'Yes, Inspector.'

'That is better. Now, outside the Property Department there are often coolies sitting on the ground waiting for orders. There are clerks also, coming and going?'

Silence.

'Are there? Are there? Yes or no?'

'Yes, Inspector.'

Yet still not a flicker in that face.

'You often go to the Property Department?'

'Sometimes, Inspector.'

Plainly a half-truth. Safe enough to risk contradicting that.

'But this morning only Manager sahib and Sub-Manager also were telling me something very different. They were saying that often and often stars are sending you when you are their stand-in to have changes made in their costumes.'

Still that downward-cast face.

'Yes or no? Yes or no? Answer up.'

'Yes, Inspector.'

A hint of a dry mouth in that whispered reply? Keep it up.

'Very good. So you are often going to the Property Department and the many coolies sitting outside know you well. Yes?'

'Yes, Inspector.'

That was better. That came quicker.

'And you know these coolies?'

'Some. Perhaps.'

It seemed as if under this grinding the fragments of fact were becoming smaller and smaller. They were hard little nuggets still, but surely the possibility of at last breaking them down till they hid nothing was there.

'You know more than one of those fellows out there by name, isn't it?'

But no answer now.

He brought his hands up on to the top of the desk and bunched them loosely into fists.

'Yes, Inspector. Yes.'

That had been an instant reaction. His spirit must have taken a battering during the night in the lock-up. There were raw areas there.

From the scatter of flat little paperweights on the desk top he selected the heaviest, and holding it in his right hand he brought it smacking down into his left palm. The sound was loud in the quiet of the little office, with only the occasional cawing of a crow or hoot of a motor-horn outside.

In the stand-in's downward-held eyes a tiny side glance betrayed that the pantomime had had its effect.

'Now, Sudhaker, it is time that you and I got down to business.'

No reply to that of course.

'Well, Sudhaker, do you agree? Yes? Yes?'

'Yes, Inspector.'

Hah, the fellow no longer knew what he was saying. In we go.

'You did not stay near the Property Department after you had taken in that turban, did you, Sudhaker?'

'Yes, Inspector. Yes, I did. Yes, yes.'

That was panic. Press in, press in.

'How dare you lie to me, my friend? How dare you? Now

then, where did you go when you had left the turban? Where? Where? Come on, out with it.'

'Inspector, nowhere.'

'Nowhere? Nowhere? You have a body, Sudhaker. You have legs and arms and a trunk. Legs and arms and a trunk that can feel pain, too, let me remind you. Now where were they, those legs and arms of yours? Nowhere? Nowhere? I do not see how that can be, my friend.'

'Inspector. Inspector . . .'

'Well, speak up. Speak up. Where did you go when you came out from leaving the turban? Dhartiraj's turban, Sudhaker? Dhartiraj's turban that he was not wearing when that Five-K crashed down on to him? Where did you go when you had left it?'

'Inspector, to make water only. Only that, I swear.'

'Oh, so you swear now, do you? You swear to your lies, to add to it all?'

'No, no, Inspector. I did that. I did. I did.'

He knew at that moment – all his experience of criminals and witnesses lying and wriggling under questioning told him so – that in this at least Sudhaker Wani was telling the truth.

It crossed his mind that the Property Department Sub-Manager had ironically proved wrong about the man's need to answer nature's calls, however much he believed him to be right about some secret core in him that seemed impervious to ordinary human weaknesses. But had he now penetrated to that core, found it was not so remarkable after all?

Certainly he had the fellow at his mercy now. And he could hold him there, just by keeping his eyes fixed on him, while he thought over the implications of this small piece of fact that he had, with disproportionate effort, pulled out.

All right, after taking in Dhartiraj's turban for its richer encrustation of jewels he had gone out to relieve himself. Where would he have gone? No doubt round some corner, perhaps up against the high surrounding wall of the Studios compound. So how much of the quite short time needed to get into Sound Stage No. 2, up that ladder and across to the Five-K would have been taken up? The distance involved was not long and the handing-over of the turban had taken only at most two minutes. How long to go and urinate? One minute? Perhaps a little longer. But that would still leave him enough time. It plainly would.

He felt the nearness of the kill run like a fiery spirit through his veins. A promise of heady intoxication soon flooding over him.

Abruptly to be stopped.

With absolute suddenness he saw that the picture he had been constructing, a picture born when Jagdish Rana had described the murderer realizing what the hanging Five-K meant and returning to the scene to take the curve-bladed dagger, scramble up the ladder, make his swaying way across the catwalk and slash at those ropes, was not true. It did not fit the sober facts of life.

Quite simply, a man who had decided to kill Dhartiraj would not have been able to stand somewhere and quietly relieve himself. It would be possible, yes, that Sudhaker had not wholly made up his mind to kill Dhartiraj when he had seen the dangling Five-K and that, torn by indecision, he had actually gone round some corner as if to urinate and had counted on his answer manifesting itself then according to some code of luck. The human mind could work like that. But it was not possible that Sudhaker had actually gone somewhere and urinated in relaxation and then had hurried off to cut down that Five-K.

And, though there was nothing in the way of proof, he himself had no doubt at all that what Sudhaker had told him was the simple truth. He had gone to a corner somewhere and had urinated.

And so he had not murdered Dhartiraj.

But there was some mystery there still. The fellow had done something that had justly put him into his present state of fear. Best find that out before anything else.

'You made water,' he said, not letting the pressure slacken by the least amount. 'And what else did you do after? That was not all. What else did you do?'

The stand-in did not answer.

'Well, you made water, and then what? Come on, you have more time to account for than that. What did you do?'

Still there was no reply. But the silence was quite different from the silences that had gone before it. Ghote could feel it. It must have been evident in some tiny difference of stance or perhaps even in the rate of breathing, though he would have been hard put to it to pin down just what it was. But he knew quite clearly that this was no longer the resolute indifference of the Haunted Palace interview and neither was it at all the evasive silences of the beginning of this interrogation. It was the silence of desperation, pure desperation.

It would not take long to break.

'Where, Sudhaker? Where?'

And that barked demand was enough.

'Sahib. Inspector. I was talking with Salim Ali. He is a young fellow, Inspector, who is working as extra and is also sometimes a musician with a hotel band. And, Inspector, he writes songs. They are very good – That – That is, Inspector, they may be quite good. And I wished to buy one.'

'To buy a song?'

He felt himself slithering helplessly, deprived of all sense of direction. Only the fact that the stand-in had checked himself after saying that the young Muslim's songs were 'very good' had told him that, however unlikely it might seem, Sudhaker believed himself to be revealing a secret that was valuable indeed. And this was enough to keep him hammering.

'To buy a song, man? What is this? Speak up, speak up.'

'Inspector, for a film.'

The stand-in spoke the words in such a tone of beaten-down confession – they had hardly been audible at all – that Ghote knew at once that he had penetrated to the fellow's innermost secret.

'Go on,' he said simply.

'Inspector, this is for what I have been making every anna I could. This is why I was selling Durga Auntie's spells and mixtures. This was why I was helping to run blue-film shows and selling smuggled items and hanging round the stars' *chumchas* making black-money deals and listening for little things to sell

93

to the gossip writers. Inspector, did you think it was to get cash for spending only? No, to make a film you are needing capital outlay. Enough at least to buy something good going cheap, like Salim Ali's songs when he is wanting always money for *bhang* and other drug – Enough to buy, if you can, a good song, Inspector, so that you can borrow enough to make six-eight reels to show to the distributors and in that way make a beginning.'

Ghote blinked in astonishment.

'You are aiming to be a producer, a film producer?' he asked.

His evident incredulity roused the stand-in.

'Any why not?' he spat out. 'Why not, please? Did not Seth Chagan Lal begin from nowhere himself? And is he not a true *crorepati* now?'

'Yes,' Ghote said slowly, his exchanges with the wealth-oozing Seth clear in his mind. 'Yes, I see that you may be right.'

He saw more. He saw, with this explanation of the stand-in's behaviour, that the path he had been following in his eager hunt for Dhartiraj's killer had finally come to its destination. And that destination had nothing at all to do with murder.

He had been on a long, long detour. And, worse, now that he had retraced his steps and come back to the place he had turned off wrongly, there was, with Jagdish Rana's motive brutally removed by the laughing Seth Chagan Lal, nowhere else at all to go.

Life had flicked off the switch of the great stairway of light up which he had thought he was climbing. And there was suddenly no upward path left. Only blackness.

He sat on at his desk after he had ordered Sudhaker Wani to be taken away and let the dismal grey clouds sweep endlessly across his mind, barren of even the least drop of life-giving rain.

Every hope had dwindled to extinction. Sudhaker Wani had turned out to be no more than a mixed-bag petty criminal with ridiculous ambitions. Jagdish Rana's once naked motive had been shrivelled up by Seth Chagan Lal's dismissive laughter. And with the ever-friendly ever-liked Dhartiraj as victim there were, unlikely as it might seem, simply no other suspects. His long talk with Miss Officewalla had shown him that. If anyone had ever known anything to the detriment of a star, Miss Officewalla would have told him of it. That was something certain in a world of fantasy.

But no one she had told him about – except, of course, the great Ravi Kumar, who had not been in the Studios when Dhartiraj had died – appeared to have had the least motive for the murder.

For a few hallucinatory moments he toyed with the notion of somehow proving that, after all, Ravi Kumar had entered the Studios. In disguise? But he was a star and could not possibly have passed the scrutiny of the chowkidars unnoticed. At tremendous speed? But the gates were shut, and however fast a star flashed by in his Mercedes or big Buick he would be seen and saluted. By some other entrance? But there was none. A high wall surrounded the whole Studios compound and there was only one way in, and besides a star could not enter in stealth. No, in saying Ravi Kumar was a star, a superstar, everything was said. A superstar did not commit murder, could not commit murder. The two ideas just did not belong in the same world. A superstar up in the Court of Sessions on a murder charge. You might as well bring a civil action against one of the gods.

So what was left? Nothing.

What had become of all his hopes? Where was the promise of stardom as a detective? What had happened to the fiery pledge he had given Nilima, Nilima, brightest female ornament of the starry heaven as Ravi Kumar was its brightest male ornament? That burning promise had died into nothingness. Utter nothingness.

Sitting at his familiar desk, staring at the door in front of him, he could feel that word echoing and mocking through the empty spaces of his head. Nothing, nothing, nothing. Until quite suddenly he realized that there was in that desolate terrain one tiny contradictory form.

In the rolling hills reverberating with that empty thunder there was one small upright figure. It was duty. Routine. The insignificant yet undeniable demand of his calling.

He had a report to make out.

He heaved his typewriter on to the desk, took paper and carbons from their drawer, inserted them, checked peeringly that the carbon was the right way round, poised the forefingers of either hand to type and began.

There were, at least, all the technical aspects to the case to deal with. The police surgeon's conclusions from the post-mortem, though they added nothing to what he had conjectured himself, the painstaking findings of the scene-of-crime technicians, for all that they did no more than confirm what had been perfectly evident at first sight, even the fact that there were only the fingerprints of the correct Lights Boy on the remains of the smashed Five-K, all had to be incorporated in their proper order.

He sat for a moment then and wondered whether he ought to move on to give an account of what had actually been his first step in the case, his interview with Seth Chagan Lal. Surely not. What the Seth had had to say had been nothing really to do with the matter.

Yet the thought of the Seth filled him with a sudden inexplicable disquiet. He pulled out a handkerchief to dab at his abruptly sweat-damp neck.

Well, at least what the Seth had said about Jagdish Rana was relevant. He battered furiously at the typewriter keys setting it out.

But at last the whole course of his investigation up to that minute was there on paper. And not a single conclusion had emerged. Not even the hint of some new lead.

There was only one thing to be done. Go through the whole pile of banged-at sheets and smudgy carbons and correct all the typing errors.

He took an old blue ballpoint from the little brass tray in front of him and set to work.

It was only when he had got right through to reading over what he had written about Sudhaker Wani and the stand-in's unimpressive features rose again in his mind's eye that a chance remark the fellow had made suddenly jutted up in the smooth run of the routine like a little jagged thorn.

It had been when the fellow was finally admitting the many ways in which he raised money towards his extraordinary aim of becoming a producer. He had mentioned gathering little scraps of gossip to sell from the stars' *chumchas*. And it was just this thought of *chumchas* that turned his own mind now to considering Dhartiraj's leaderless crew. No doubt Miss Officewalla had been right in telling him that for any one of them to have murdered Dhartiraj would have been killing the goose that laid the golden eggs. But had there not been one name in that list she had brought out with such impressive speed which was a little different from the others? Had there not been a young man attached to Dhartiraj, but not one of his regular *chumchas*? A well-off young fellow the big star had met at a charity cricket match up in Delhi and had brought back to Bombay? Had brought back with promises of stardom in his turn? Promises which had not been kept.

But how much had Dhartiraj really tried to fulfil those promises? Had he not perhaps promised everything and done nothing? So was there not then in his circle someone with a grievance against him, a strong grievance?

What was the young man's name?

He dived into his piles of notes. Sheets of paper rose into the air, slipped to this side, slithered to that, fluttered down on to the floor. His hands padded and clutched.

And then he had the list he wanted. And there at the end of it was the name.

Kishore Sachdev.

Yes. That was it. That was him.

And, as he stared at the two words scrawled on the battered sheet of paper, creased and crumpled from its long sojourn in his shirt pocket, the whole idea of the youngster as Dhartiraj's murderer grew and flowered in his mind.

He saw the whole situation. A young man in Delhi, well-off but bored in the sterile atmosphere of the capital with its endless concern over status, its intrigues, its small circle of people meeting and meeting each other at parties and receptions, at clubs and restaurants. And then into that never-ending round would have come the splendid rosy promise.

Stardom. A life of glamour. Of renown. Of recognition through all the length and breadth of India. Of adulation.

It would seem like a dream happening in reality. There would be the flight to Bombay sitting beside the friendly already established star and the heart beating and thudding over every mile of the journey.

And then in Bombay over the months there would come the slow fizzing-away of hope. Disillusion. Then bitterness.

Yes, by God, that young man might very well long to kill Dhartiraj. But had he been in the Studios at the time of the murder?

Even Assistant Inspector Jahdev had not yet been able to produce a complete list of every person whatsoever who had been inside the high walls of the compound when Dhartiraj had died. There were dozens of coolies and Ghati women it would take days to trace and account for. But it was so unlikely that any one of them would have killed Dhartiraj that the effort was hardly worthwhile. A person like Kishore Sachdev, on the other hand, would almost certainly be recorded as having been present if he had been there.

Once more the papers on the desk rose and fell.

And then there it was. The name on the list. 'Kishore Sachdev, model'.

Dhartiraj had not been accompanied to the Studios on the morning of his murder by many of his entourage. But this young man had gone along. Perhaps to make one more plea to the influential star for a small starring part of his own. He had been there.

Rising like a waterspout gradually mounting far out to sea, Ghote felt within him the increasing pressure of excitement. He was on to something. And it was something that no one else had in the least thought of. Not Miss Officewalla, for all her knowledge of the *filmi duniya*, though it had been from her that he had learnt the key fact. Not Assistant Inspector Jahdev, for all his lists and inquiries. Not Seth Chagan Lal, for all his onward-rushing determination. Not Jagdish Rana, for all his efforts to get himself off the hook. Not Sudhaker Wani, for all the little pieces of knowledge he dug for round the Studios.

No, he himself, the star investigator, had picked out this tiny thread when all the others had gone blindly looking everywhere else.

Yes, Kishore Sachdev. He had picked him out. And where was he? Where was he now?

He reached for the telephone.

Chapter 11

It took more than a little telephoning, however, to locate Kishore Sachdev. But to Ghote it seemed now that every fresh obstacle was there only to be smashed down. The man who had been selected above all the officers of Crime Branch to investigate the death of a star was not going to be prevented from getting hold of his suspect by any difficulties. Eventually he tracked down one of the young man's *filmi* friends who was usefully talkative. Yes, Kishore had gone to the Nataraj Studios at Andheri. He had gone to ask the great Ravi Kuma for a side-hero's role in the huge new multi-star mystery movie *Grand Trunk Express men Hatya* which the superstar had just signed for, not only as leading player but also 'to make his bow at the megaphone', since he had seen the original in the UK and could, with the help of a cameraman 'to look after angles and things like that', make a shot-for-for-shot hit out of it.

So it was not until well into the afternoon, after another distinctly exhilarating encounter with the Press – 'I am actively pursuing an important new lead' – that he found himself at last at the Nataraj Studios.

Somewhere in the back lot he emerged unexpectedly from a clutter of buildings very similar to those at Talkiestan into what he at once realized was a typical Indian village. All down the slope of a small hillock a beaten-earth village street had been created. On each side little mud-built houses looked out, their doorways none the less dark for the fact that they backed on to either the high wire fence of the Studios compound or on to the walls of a sound stage. Artfully arranged freshly-cut branches ingeniously blocked out the intrusive corners of other buildings and at one point a whole mock palm rose up especially to conceal – Ghote felt a jab of pleasure at realizing this – the top of a telegraph pole.

At the foot of this immemorially typical street stood a camera on a tripod. It was backed by a large row of canvas chairs occupied by the Director of this film – Ghote had not been able to find out what it was called, but he had learnt from Kishore Sachdev's friend that it was one of twenty-seven which the great Ravi Kumar was at present engaged upon – and other prominent actors, including at the far end none other than Nilima again, sitting beside an elderly lady who from her proud looks and considerable amplitude could only be her mother. At the star's feet a tailor knelt stitching furiously at sequins round the hem of her peasant skirt.

Nilima, he thought. Nilima here. Nilima here to witness the arrest. My pledge to her kept right before her eyes. And then . . . Then when the trial had been brought to a successful end amid the full dazzle of nation-wide publicity, then Nilima's gratitude, Nilima's friendship. A new and totally different life. It could be. It would be. It must be.

He directed a probing, furious glare at the small crowd of people standing behind the chairs. Kishore Sachdev should be among them. But he did not know what the young aspirant to stardom looked like and abruptly too much was happening elsewhere for it to be possible for him to make inquiries.

Never mind. He could wait. What he had come here for was worth waiting to achieve.

What had caused the sudden flurry of activity had been the appearance at the top of the little hill of the great superstar himself, mounted in full glory upon a superbly bejewelled riding saddle fixed to the back of an ancient sports car. He was dressed in a richly embroidered kurta and his head was held high, the famous cutting profile, which Ghote had seen on hundreds of huge hoardings and on thousands of bright-coloured posters, looking down proudly on the scene below. Almost under his nose another cameraman crouched on the front of the car, held in place by two straining assistants. On either side, appallingly insecure, coolies clung on holding wide sheets of reflecting metal to catch and intensify the light of the sun.

'Silence,' yelled the Director.

'Silence, silence,' a score of voices clamorously echoed.

And, when at last silence was achieved, 'Camera!' the Director shouted.

A Clapper Boy jumped forward and held his board in front of the camera's nose. It clicked resoundingly. 'Action.'

The old sports car slid forward down the hill, skilfully manoeuvring between the house fronts on either side of the narrow earthen path. Ravi Kumar rode with marvellous dash, reins held with contemptuous looseness, whip crackingly flourished. Two-thirds of the way down the little hill he pulled up with a magnificent toss of his head. He turned a little in the saddle and haughtily regarded the dark house doorway on his left.

'Cut! Cut!'

A look of mean rage flashed on to the famous profile.

'Raviji,' the Director called out. 'You must not come so far down before you see the girl in the doorway of that hut. Otherwise when we shoot Nilima there the background would not be the same.'

Ravi Kumar brought his whip thwacking down on the front of the car.

'Directorji,' he shouted. 'You have made me start too far forward. Am I having to teach you your business also?'

The Director hopped to his feet and hurried a little way up the hill.

'It is that damned setting coolie, Raviji,' he explained. 'He was altogether misplacing the mark. You. You there. Where are you?'

From the darkness of one of the doorways up against the high outside fence of the compound a bare-chested coolie emerged.

'Adjust the stone of Mr Ravi Kumar,' the Director ordered in a voice of thunder.

The coolie trotted up the hill to a point where a large white stone appeared to have been carelessly left by the roadside. He turned.

'But – But –' he could be heard to mutter.

The Director straightened himself to his full height. Rage contorted his every feature.

'Are you daring to tell that that stone was put where I ordered?' he yelled. 'If Mr Ravi Kumar is saying it is in the wrong place it is in the wrong place. Move it. Move it.'

'But – '

'Move it or never enter these Studios again.'

The coolie stooped and picked up the stone. He set off step by step down the hill, pausing at each one to see whether it was the spot where he ought to lay down his burden.

'More. More. Idiot. Idiot.'

The Director actually jumped from the ground in the wildness of his rage.

At last the coolie put the stone down.

'No, you fool,' the Director yelled yet more loudly. 'Not so far. Back. Back. Up. Up.'

The coolie picked the stone up and climbed back up the hill.

'There.'

Ravi Kumar himself had pronounced the word.

'There, there,' the Director yelled. 'There, where I was all along saying.'

He walked backwards till he reached his chair and flopped into it in utter exhaustion.

Then, with much shouting of directions and counter-directions, the old car was carefully reversed up the little hill till once more it was at the crest.

'Silence,' called the Director with what was left of his voice.

'Silence,' Ravi Kumar shouted from the hill-top.

'Silence,' respectfully echoed voice after voice.

And the shooting of the scene began again. The old car started to glide forward. Ravi Kumar sat up more straightly in his saddle. He flourished his whip.

But hardly had the car advanced ten yards when it became clearly evident to everybody that the marker stone at which Ravi Kumar was to begin to bring his horse to a rearing halt was in totally the wrong position for him to look into the correct house doorway at the end of the manoeuvre.

'Cut! Cut! Cut! Cut!' the Director yelled, as if by sheer repetition he could somehow obliterate the plain fact that the stone was ridiculously too far down.

But his yelling did nothing to avert the superstar's wrath.

He jumped down from his high saddle in one lithe bound. He strode down the rest of the hill towards the Director in ominous silence. And then he exploded.

'Please be so good as to tell me how it is possible for an artiste to perform in conditions like these. How can he? Where is his art? How can he build up a truly great performance when all the time people are doing things like this to him?'

The Director very slowly rose from his chair, crouching a little as if to keep under a line of fire.

Ravi Kumar planted himself right in front of him.

'You are doing it so as to make my role a failure,' he shouted. 'They are bribing you because they cannot stand somebody having six-seven hit-films one after the other. But I am not going to let it happen. I am not staying here to be insulted. I am going. Yes, going. Now. Now. Now.'

But he did not go. He stayed long enough to repeat all he had said previously and to add one or two more observations. And only then did he turn on his heel and march away.

From behind the row of chairs a whole flock of men hurried forward, chattering like so many sparrows, and set off in the superstar's wake. The *chumchas*, Ghote thought, pleased with his quickness. Yes, they would be following to add their agreement to everything the enraged Ravi Kumar said, to suggest what they could to make his fury burn yet higher, even to offer themselves as targets for its side blows. He saw it all.

And then he saw that a well-dressed young man was following the chattering flock at a slight distance, looking anxiously towards the striding superstar almost as if he was a foreign-exchange tout waiting a favourable opportunity to descend on some rich tourist.

Kishore Sachdev.

It could be no one else.

Swiftly he set out after him. He felt, as he rapidly closed on him, the throb of the hunter's excitement. The unknown they had all left out of account, the one person who had a good motive for wanting to kill the all-popular Dhartiraj. And he had him under his claws.

'Kishore Sachdev.'

The young man wheeled round, the very picture of guilt. Almost there and then he put him under arrest.

But no. Question him. Get the facts out of him. Get, if it looked at all possible, a confession. And then the path of glory could begin. The making certain of the case, the trial, the final sentence, the acclaim.

He looked closely at the young hopeful whom Dhartiraj had brought from Delhi with such empty promises. He was, he saw, at most twenty-two or twenty-three. Tall, handsome enough, with good strong features and a well-fleshed face. Yes, the basic equipment for stardom, to judge by what the accepted stars looked like. And the eyes. They were large and a limpid brown, reflecting at this moment, clearly as the still surface of a jungle pool, all that the fellow must be feeling, bewilderment, fear and – surely – guilt.

He watched his every least reaction like a crouching panther.

'Mr Sachdev, my name is Ghote, Inspector Ghote, CID. I am in charge of the investigation into the death of Dhartiraj.'

Would there appear something new in those large pool-reflecting eyes? The dull acknowledgement that a daring plan had not after all been successful?

He had to record that nothing of this sort appeared. Perhaps the boy was a bit more of a tough customer than he looked. But one good long hard session across a desk, and he would be finished. He had the marks of soft living all over him, the just thickening roll of flesh at the neck, the beautifully kept finger-nails, the well-oiled hair, elaborately cut. Yes, he would snap all right. Snap at a touch.

'I have a number of questions to put to you, Mr Sachdev, in connection with my inquiries.'

The boy licked at his thick sensuous top lip.

'To me? To me, Inspector? But . . .'

'Yes, to you, Mr Sachdev. And why not? Can you tell me that: why not to you?'

Kishore Sachdev swallowed.

He could trace it as if in a slow-motion film, the nervous jerk of the Adam's apple.

By God, he would get him here and now, just where they were. No need of the trappings of an official interrogation.

He turned and gave the hastiest of glances back to the row of chairs at the foot of the little hill. Nilima, was she there still? She was. But she was listening, head gracefully bent, to something her mother was saying. Laying down the law, by the look of it. What could he do to attract her attention?

He could think of nothing.

He turned back to Kishore Sachdev. To be confronted by the calm and easy look of the well-off, of the people for whom the police were respectful protectors, if not simple servants.

Inwardly he cursed himself. If only he had struck while he had the running . . .

But it was no use wishing. That moment of triumph, with Nilima first among the audience, was not to happen now.

'Mr Sachdev,' he said, making his voice as stiff and un-yielding as he could, 'I must ask you to accompany me to Head-quarters. I have reason to believe you can be of material assistance in my investigation.'

The boy looked back at him calmly. He guessed that he was weighing up whether he should pretend to assert himself with all the arrogance of the rich or to be falling in with this little policeman's whim. He would, damn him, be coolly working out which of the two attitudes was most likely to help him conceal what he had to hide.

Well, let him choose whichever he cared to. The realities of an interrogation would soon produce an altogether different story.

'Inspector, I will happily answer your every question. But I have important business here at Nataraj, so could we not go somewhere quiet here?'

What was this? What was he trying? Was it no more than an attempt to make things easier for himself by choosing a favour-able setting? Or was there some other reason?

In any case there was no question of agree –

He checked himself.

No, better to let the young upstart think he had gained something. Then when the chips came down he would be all the more disconcerted.

'Very well.'

'Let me think . . . Ah yes, there is Mr Kumar's dressing-room. I was with him there before the shooting. He will certainly not come back to the Studios for a little now, so we can go there.'

'Very well,' Ghote said again.

He felt nevertheless quite put out. The casual ease with which the young would-be star proposed to make use of the dressing-room of such a distantly high figure as Ravi Kumar made him feel acutely the difference there was between the two of them. He himself, he knew well, would never have dreamed even of asking permission. Yet this well-off youngster had just assumed the right.

He followed him through the confusion of huts and buildings that made up the Studios.

Yet Ravi Kumar's dressing-room proved to be not at all what he had expected. It was small. It was very untidy. It did not even smell very pleasant, even though a bottle of Yardley's after-shave stood with its cap off on the cluttered dressing-table.

The dressing-table, with its square mirror surrounded by bare light bulbs, was altogether a terrible mess. Ashtrays full of butts lay here and there on its glass surface mingled with half-empty teacups and squashed packets of cigarettes, Dunhill and other expensive foreign brands. A three-quarter-melted bowl of ice had had some chewed *paan* spat into it.

On the floor there were even two or three gnawed chicken bones among the empty and half-empty Limca, Coca-Cola and Mangola bottles and the full ashtrays. And plainly no one had bothered themselves to heed the painted notice on the bathroom door saying 'Please Try to Leave Clean'. That strong sour odour was all too apparently coming from there.

There were, however, plenty of chairs in the confined space. Ghote took one and indicated another to Kishore Sachdev. And he found, as he sat down, that something – it was most probably the atmosphere of the sordid little dressing-room – had taken all the fizz out of him. He addressed the young man opposite soberly.

'Please be so good as to tell me where you were yesterday morning between the hours of nine and eleven ack emma.'

'But, Inspector, you must know. I was at Talkiestan Studios. I went there with Dhartiraj. There were times when he did not want a whole crowd with him, and then often he would ask me only to come.'

A little surprised by this frankness, Ghote went resolutely on.

'He asked you only. Why was that, Mr Sachdev? Were you very close to him?'

The large limpid eyes clouded, as if the boy found the question particularly difficult to answer.

'Well?' Ghote prompted carefully.

'Inspector, I think it was because I was different. I was not one of his *chumchas*. From me he could expect true answers.'

He had been about to press in with another question. But some faint extra look of anxiety had come into the boy's eyes with those last words, and he restrained himself.

'Well, no, that is not exactly correct,' the boy said.

Ghote waited.

He was not sure where these hesitant answers were leading – they were certainly not going in the direction he had expected when he had first told the young man he wanted to question him – but it was clear that there was something here bursting to be said. And that was worth any amount of patient waiting for.

The silence grew.

Then, with a look of overwhelming trouble welling up into his telltale eyes, Kishore Sachdev came out with it.

'No. When you get down to it in the end, I was altogether no better than any of them. I also wanted what Dhartiraj had in his gift, and in my way I did as much as any of those *chumchas* who were hoping to be given a little flat or a car or a good dinner at the Taj even. I also told him lies. I also said what I thought he would want to hear, and I did not mind if there was nothing of the truth in it at all.'

Ghote stamped hard on the tinges of pity that had grown

responsively in him. The scent of the hunt was beginning to rise from the ground ahead again and he was not going to let it go.

'You lied to Dhartiraj,' he barked out. 'You cheated him. And that must mean that you hated him. You hated him, isn't it? You hated Dhartiraj.'

He glared hard at those pool-eyes. In them now he was going to see an admission. An admission that, yes, the boy had hated the dead star. And after that would come the beginnings of a confession. A confession to seizing on that suddenly appearing opportunity, to snatching the curve-bladed dagger, to running up the ladder to the catwalk, to cutting the ropes of the Five-K and watching it fall.

And, just as he had counted on, it came, the look in those eyes that said clearly as any jabber of gabbled-out words 'Yes, I hated Dhartiraj'.

'I wanted to hide it,' the boy whispered. 'I feared that I would be asked, and I wanted to hide it. But you have got it out of me, Inspector. Oh God, so soon.'

Ghote felt it singing and singing inside him. The triumph. Yes, he had got it out of this boy quickly. But then he was the man to do that. He had been chosen for just this task. This was his case and he had cracked it, and soon there would come the courtroom, the listening judge, the gowned pleaders and the star prosecution witness. And after that . . . After that the flash and dazzle of the photographers' light-bulbs and then the long newspaper articles. 'How I Brought A Star's Killer to Justice, by Ganesh V. Ghote.'

Chapter 12

Ghote sat more straightly on his chair amid the clutter and mess of Ravi Kumar's little sour-smelling dressing-room. Kishore Sachdev, opposite him, was sitting heavily slumped, his well-fleshed shoulders sagging, his pool-limpid eyes clearly signalling the turmoil within.

Ghote spoke decisively.

'Just tell me everything.'

His notepad was ready. His ballpoint poised.

Again it was the wretched pink thing he had bought in a hurry one day from a pavement vendor's array. But no matter. Soon it would be nothing but proper fountain-pens carefully chosen in proper pen marts.

'Come, tell.'

Kishore Sachdev raised his head a little. His eyes shone with a pure desire to unburden himself.

'Inspector,' he said, almost as if he was only half-conscious of the words beginning to pour out. 'I met Dhartiraj first when I was in hotel management line in Delhi. You know my parents are rich. My father wanted me to follow him in contracting business. But I did not at all like that idea. So he persuaded me to go into hotel line. And I met Dhartiraj when he stayed in the hotel where I was. He allowed me to take him to dinner, and after I saw him again and again. And I told him that it had always been my ambition-ambition to be a star.'

He paused. In his limpid eyes Ghote saw all that was conjured up for him by the word 'star'. An existence in another world, free from all the dust and trappings of that everyday world in which children, however pampered, are brought up and go to school and meet with disappointments, and where young men, however much money there is at their disposal, encounter the snags and difficulties of ordinary living, the constant failure to achieve what the eager mind has foreseen. That was what 'star' would have meant: a wonderful world of nothing ever being less than what it might have been.

For a moment his attention focused on the untidy sour-smelling mess that surrounded them. The spat-out *paan* had coloured all the melted water in the ice-bowl now, a pale rusty red. And this was the actual world of the biggest star of them all. But that was a thought to be pushed aside.

'Go on,' he said, curbing his urgency with difficulty.

Kishore Sachdev began again, in the same dreamy voice as if he was hauling up buckets of remembrance from a deep well.

'When – when I told him I wanted and wanted to be a star, he at once invited me to come to Bombay. He was very warm. We

109

shall be brothers, he said. So I told my father that I wanted to go and there was a terrible-terrible row, and my mother was in tears also. But I left. And in Bombay at first it seemed to be as it had been in Delhi. Always there was a role for me just around the corner. Always Dhartiraj was repeating I was altogether handsome enough for a star, that my voice was very good, that I dressed very well. But then the right chance was never quite coming. Each time there was something wrong. And in the meanwhile I am entertaining that man. I am giving him daily a thousand salutes. I am taking him to the Taj, to Sheraton also. Wining and dining, booted and suited. The only thing I was not doing was getting girls for him. And it was a long, long time.'

The flow hesitated and stopped. The boy sat brooding on some inner vision.

'How long altogether?' Ghote prompted.

'How long?'

'Yes, how long since you came from Delhi?'

'Oh, that has been more than two years.'

'And what have you been doing all this time?' Ghote asked, stung into curiosity. 'Nothing but entertain Dhartiraj?'

'No. No, I did other things.'

He paused, still inward-turned. Ghote was on the point of giving him a push when he began again.

'No, I am taking some modelling work. They also say I am very good and will one day become a star.'

'But did you not get any acting roles at all?'

'Well, you must understand that, if your ultimate aim is to reach the grade – top one, if God is willing – then it is not right to take any small parts. Then you would become an actor only. But one side-hero's part I got, the Villain's brother. It was not very long ago. The film has not been shown yet.'

'I must go and see it when it comes out,' Ghote said.

And underneath he thought 'What a hit it will be, with a murderer playing in it.'

'There is nothing to see,' Kishore Sachdev said, with a flicker of fire. 'In the cutting-room every foot of that part was taken out. I had thought that my break had come, that for once a star was not using an actor beside him that he knew would not make

110

an outstanding impression, that for once a star was not using his nephew or his son.'

The pool-eyes were burning now.

'But, Inspector, he sat there in the cutting-room telling the Director what to take out. He had seen the rushes, Inspector. I also. And I was too good. That was a rich field to project my histrionics. And he would not have.'

'But I thought he was always very friendly,' Ghote objected.

'But he was a star, Inspector. He would not have another role eating into his own. And he was friendly all the time, too. He said it would spoil the film having two Villains. So my part must go and another song be put in instead.'

The boy sank into silence, a silence seething and bubbling underneath with pricking resentment.

'You hated him for that,' Ghote stated, 'and so you killed him.'

'No.'

For a few instants Ghote truly believed that he had misheard the single syllable the boy had spoken. He was even about to prompt him to expand on the one word of his confession to the murder when the realization of what had actually been said came home to him.

'No?' he said. 'No? You are denying that you killed him? Come, what is the use? Already you have told me so much, make a clean breast of it all now. It is the only way.'

'But I did not kill him,' the boy repeated.

Then Ghote felt the anger surge up in him, a great black monster power-driven through the sea, on the point of breaking through and destroying.

He hurled himself to his feet, thrust his face down at the fleshily handsome boy's.

'I know very well you killed Dhartiraj,' he shouted, his face right up close to those well-fed features. 'I know it. You need not think you are going to get away with this. I tell you, I know too much. Now, answer up. You killed him?'

As near as he was to the boy's big brown eyes he could see the least flicker in them. And it was plain that his shouting was having its effect. The boy was frightened, scared out of his wits.

He waited for the confession.

The boy's tongue, thick and pink, came out and licked quickly at his lips.

'Inspector, I did not. I did not.'

'You dare to lie to me. I will have you stripped to nothing for this. To nothing. Do you understand? Do not go thinking anybody or anything will protect you. Now, out with it. You saw that Five-K hanging, you went up there, you cut the ropes. Out with it.'

'No, no. I tell you a thousand times "no". I did not do it. I hated that man, yes. I came to hate him, and I hated him all the more because he was my only hope. But I did not kill him. I did not.'

The rage bucked and jumped in Ghote's mind, strong, heavy, thwacking.

'You will not get away with this, young Sachdev. I am going to make it hell for you, double hell. You think you can lie and wriggle your way out of this. But let me tell you one thing. Not all the money you can bring, not all the lawyers, will help you one little bit. This is the murder of a star. A star. The whole damn world is against you and I am at the head of it.'

He saw the face, still within inches of his own, cringe and crumple.

'Now,' he shouted, 'the details. Each and every detail, and quick about it.'

'No. No. No. No.'

The boy was shouting back now, shouting back desperately. Flecks of spittle came up and spattered against his own face, frothy and faintly cool.

And in those large limpid truth-telling eyes he saw that what he was shouting was so.

The boy had not murdered Dhartiraj. He knew that now at last, with as much certainty as if a hundred witnesses had lined up in front of him and each had repeated that they had seen the boy ten miles from the scene.

He sat back in his chair and let a long sigh whistle out.

'Were you near Dhartiraj at Talkiestan?' he asked, careless almost of the answer.

112

'Inspector, I was with him up until he sent that stand-in fellow to get more jewels on that turban. Then, when he said he would go through his dialogues, I left.'

'You did not hear his dialogues for him?'

A little spark of hope had come back to him, flickering delusively. Surely it would be the duty of whoever was with a star to do that for him? Was there something here after all out of character?

'No, Inspector. That I did not do. His *chumchas*, yes. They knew that going over dialogues was one of the things they had to do because he did not read well.'

'But if he did not read?' Ghote said, the flickering light still dancing and faltering in the darkness ahead.

'Inspector, it was not that he could not read. It was just that he did not like. When he nearly knew his dialogues he could follow them without trouble.'

A sudden memory rose inconsequently in Ghote's head, empty and purposeless as it was now rapidly becoming. Another star who had had difficulty over reading something. Nilima. She had asked him to read one of his lists aloud to her. Disillusionment swept across him.

'Nilima also?' he asked before he could stop himself. 'She cannot read?'

The boy looked up at him, a little surprised.

'Yes,' he said, 'Nilima can read. With her it is that she refuses always to wear specs.'

Ghote thrust away this new lost illusion. He ought to be pursuing that flickering hope of there being something not quite explained in what the boy had told him.

'But all the same,' he said, 'it might have been what you would be asked to do, to hear Dhartiraj's dialogues for that scene upon the *gaddi*?'

'No,' the boy answered. 'I never did that. I was his friend.'

A sudden look of bitter self-hatred sprang into those limpid eyes.

'No, that is not so. It was that he believed I was his friend.'

With that, the last flicker of hope died. Wearily, Ghote completed his questions for form's sake.

'You left him then when he began to learn his dialogues. Where did you go?'

'Inspector, to get a cup of tea. But . . .'

'What but?'

'But when I got outside I knew that I did not want tea. I had wanted only not to be with Dhartiraj.'

'So what did you do?'

'I went and sat in his car, Inspector. It was parked well in the shade. I could be alone there.'

'Yes, I see. And did anyone come up and speak with you while you were there?'

'No. That car is air-conditioned. I left the glasses up, and they are of blue glass. No one would see.'

He looked at Ghote again.

'Inspector, I realize I am not able to give you any alibi for myself. But, Inspector, what I have said is so. I did not kill Dhartiraj.'

No, Ghote thought soberly, you did not. Certainly, you could have done. You could even have slipped out of that car, suddenly unable to resist the temptation that had come to you when you had realized how easily that Five-K could be cut down. You could have run back to Sound Stage No. 2 and climbed up to that catwalk. You could have done. But you did not.

He pushed himself to his feet.

'All right,' he said, 'that is all. I hope I have not prevented you from seeing Mr Ravi Kumar.'

The boy raised his shirtsleeve and looked at the thin gold watch on his wrist in an almost casual manner, as if those few normal words of inquiry had at once lifted him back into his ordinary life.

'Well, if I have missed him now,' he said, 'I can see him tonight. There is a big birthday party for Billy Banker at the Taj. He will be there. Everybody will be there.'

He sighed.

Ghote sat on when he had left, thinking almost idly about the interview. Really the way the boy had failed to produce any alibi was another point in his favour. If he had been doing what

114

he said he had, sitting behind the blued-glass windows of Dhartiraj's big car, then no one would have seen him. He should not have been able to produce an alibi. Indeed, the very fact of not having an alibi was yet another bonus point for him. When a murder was committed it was not really very likely that everyone who might have some reason for wishing the victim dead should have an incontrovertible alibi. And of the three people he had interviewed as likely suspects only Kishore Sachdev had simply said that he was on his own at the time Dhartiraj had died. Both Sudhaker Wani and the failing Jagdish Rana had tried in their different ways to wriggle themselves out of such a situation.

With the stand-in that was perhaps to be expected. After all, he lived on the edge of the law scraping together the money he needed to start off as a producer. But Jagdish Rana was different. He should not have tried to pretend there were people who had seen him when there had not been.

He jumped up and began to pace up and down the little room, steering clear only by instinct of the ashtrays, the gnawed bones and the bottles on the floor.

Jagdish Rana had gone further than trying to make up for himself an alibi out of nothing. He had gone out of his way to suggest that Sudhaker Wani was the murderer. Now, why? Why?

In his excitement over discovering Kishore Sachdev, this had not occurred to him. But it had been an act of the basest kind. The fellow had deliberately suggested that Sudhaker Wani, who although he was no innocent was not in fact guilty of murder, was someone who ought to be investigated, someone who ought to be arrested, tried, even in the end found guilty and hanged.

It was foul. Despicable.

The man who had done a thing like that might well indeed have done it only to avoid finding himself on trial and convicted. Convicted of murdering Dhartiraj, not so as to open the way for himself back to stardom through getting the part of Maqbet in *Khoon Ka Gaddi*, but for some other reason. Yes, some as yet undiscovered reason which he had foolishly risked having brought to light when he had uttered that, as it had turned out totally ridiculous, boast about Seth Chagan Lal.

He swung on his heel and went out. His vehicle was where he had left it, the driver lying dozing across the back seat with both doors open to give himself air. He woke him with a tap on the thigh.

'Home now,' he said. 'But come for me again at eight pip emma. I shall be going to the Taj Hotel. To a party. A *filmi* party, where everybody will be coming.'

Chapter 13

As the car zipped through the night along the sweep of Marine Drive, the coolness of the air from the sea a sheer treat, Ghote found that he was possessed by nothing of that almost insane excitement which had gripped him burningly when he had been on his way to wrench Kishore Sachdev from among the great Ravi Kumar's *chumchas*. Then, convinced that he was on the very point of seizing the murderer of Dhartiraj, he had felt himself a king. Now, the different disillusionments of that interview well in his mind, he was no more than a man with a discrepancy to clear up.

There was something unsatisfactory in what that failed star Jagdish Rana had told him. It was worth getting hold of him, even if it meant approaching him in the middle of a party at the Taj Hotel, to clear the matter up as rapidly as possible.

Yet it was conceivable that, pressed over what exactly he had been doing at the time of the murder, the bitter star would reveal that he had indeed tried to direct the hunt on to the dubious Sudhaker Wani because he saw it getting too close to himself. It was conceivable.

When the car came to a halt under the deep portico of the hotel's high tower, Ghote told the driver to park within sight over by the Gateway of India in case there might be someone to take to Headquarters later on.

In the white marbled lobby with its fountains and cool magnificence he spotted at once the person he hoped he would see, the hotel security officer. He went over and had a quiet word.

Yes, Billy Banker's birthday party was being held tonight, and, yes, if Inspector Ghote wanted one of the guests the best thing would be to mingle with the crowd, appear at this man's side and take him off without fuss.

The security officer led him up to the big reception suite where the party had just begun. He left him at the door.

'Good luck, Inspector.'

'Thank you.'

'And no disturbance?'

'None at all.'

Plainly the party was in its earliest stages. There were few enough people in the big room to be able to see at a glance that Jagdish Rana was not among them. At the far end under a cluster of bright paper lanterns the guest of honour, Billy Banker, looking just as he did in photographs and on posters, a great teeth-splattered grin all over his face, stood vigorously embracing whoever came up to him. Two or three garlands were round his neck and on his head there was a little green papier-mâché bowler hat. Happily there were enough guests between him and the doors – Was that fellow the playback singer? And those two fat men with even fatter wives in gaudy saris with all that jewellery were undoubtedly nouveau-riche film distributors – for there to be no question of going across himself to offer congratulations.

A bearer came up with an enormous tray of glasses of whisky and gin lined up in neat ranks and presided over by tall jugs of water and soda. Ghote waved him away. But he felt a flush of pure relief at having been so quickly marked down as a pukka guest. At home he had had grave fears about the smartness of his best shirt and trousers.

But he would have been even more pleased had Jagdish Rana been there already.

He told himself that his absence at this early stage of the affair by no means meant that he was not going to come. He would have to come. For any star on the edge of toppling into being only a figure from the past, to be seen at a party where 'everybody' was expected was an absolute necessity.

117

As a precaution, however, against his man arriving and running off at the sight of this policeman, he moved cautiously deeper into the huge room, already noisy with a score of different conversations under its glittering chandeliers. It was important to time his descent on the failed star just right. Suddenly the fellow would find him at his elbow, *Mr Rana, I would like a word, if you please.* Quiet, but firm. He would see then that there was no hope of getting away.

Around him the party was minute by minute gathering impetus. He glanced back at the doors. No sign of his man.

'Well, bhai, what sort of a stunt movie are you taking now?'

'No, no, it is not at all a stunt movie. Stunts it will be having, yes. But it is a folklore. Strictly a folklore.'

The voices were loud in his ear.

'Folklore, ha, ha. A flop picture before there is one reel in the cans.'

'No, no. What you are just signing for will be the flop picture. A Muslim social. Never has a Muslim social really clicked at box office.'

'But it is not at all a Muslim social. It is a Hindu picture, a devotional. You have heard altogether wrong story. I tell you, bhai, they will be going and kissing the screen when it is shown. No tout will dare sell tickets even though there are queues miles long. They will be garlanding the posters for this, garlanding the posters.'

He moved away. With all that back-slapping and shouting he would never spot Jagdish Rana if he came slipping quietly in.

The large alcoves opening off the main room were as yet mostly unoccupied. He went and stationed himself at the edge of one of them where he could get a good view of the doors and settled down to make a thorough study of the whole party. The more familiar he got with what was going on, the easier it would be when the time came to slip through the chattering gesticulating crowd and come up behind his man, quietly and efficiently as any of the bearers deftly sliding through even the most packed areas, their big trays of drinks held miraculously steady, the equally large trays of assorted snacks as adroitly balanced and twirled.

118

But one or two of those snacks would be nice now.

At home, a prey to anxiety over shirt and trousers, he had had little heart to eat the quick meal his Protima had prepared.

He must not forget, too, that he had promised her a full account of the function. But how was he to know which of the guests were stars? Those three gorgeously dressed women who had just arrived, with their heavy make-up and clustering jewellery, surely they must be stars? But which?

Through a sudden gap caused by a photographer clearing himself a space he caught a glimpse of the face of one of them. Yes, surely she had been the Vamp in the last film he had seen. Certainly the cleavage of her Western-style blouse and that pair of clinging gold-threaded pants, was very like what the Vamp had been wearing there.

Well, that would have to do for Protima.

But, if those stars had come, had Jagdish Rana as well? Had he missed him?

And if he was here it was unlikely that he would have collected the sort of admiring circle the three newcomers had gathered. Really, some of the men there were making utter fools of themselves, smiling and boasting and elbowing to get into the photographer's shots.

A bearer came by with his tray fully loaded with snacks. Their smell was deliciously mouth-watering. Oh, to take up one of those little plastic sticks, dip the morsel on the end of it into some of that spicy-looking sauce and put it into his mouth. But the bearer did not seem to notice him and he lacked the courage to call.

He pushed himself up on tiptoe so as to get a better look at the doors over the heads of the now quite dense crowd. A man was just entering whose appearance seemed familiar.

With a little sinking of awe, he realized that it was no less a person than the Chief Secretary of the State Government, the civil servant who had ultimate control over him himself. Such guests came to honour a star. And he was here under false pretences.

But Jagdish Rana was not here. Was he not going to come after all?

And if he did not, how easy would it now be to get hold of him? Had he already realized that, since no announcement had been made about Sudhaker Wani being arrested and charged with the murder of Dhartiraj, his ruse must be rebounding on his own head? Had he decided to cut and run?

Ah, there was Miss Officewalla coming in, dressed in another light green sari though one lacking the business-like pattern of squares she had been wearing the day before. He watched her stop just inside the doors and give the whole scene a slow careful survey, much as he had done himself. She was, in fact, employing just the technique he had been taught at Detective Training School. *Start from your immediate left and proceed methodically in a clockwise direction.* Yes, there was a professional all right.

And how long would it be before he had to beg her aid again in finding Jagdish Rana? And this time would he be as easy to locate as he had been out at that absurd bungalow at Juhu?

He watched Miss Officewalla advance into the crowded room, greeted every now and again with shrieking claims of deference that plainly hid a good deal of real awe. They must come, he realized, from her colleagues, or rivals, acknowledging the star of their own world. One or two of the men he had picked out earlier because of their trick, when a bearer with drinks came up, of taking one glass and swiftly tipping the contents of another into it. Miss Officewalla, he saw without surprise, was greeted knowingly by a bearer with a tray of fruit juices, and took tomato.

Well, he would let her ply her trade for a good while yet before going to ask her for help. Say a full half-hour.

He looked at his watch. Already a quarter past nine. Time had been flying.

All right then, give Jagdish Rana till ten exactly. And if he had not appeared by then, go and humbly consult the gossip queen.

People were arriving in swarms now. Men who could only be stars from their air of total assurance, though he could not even guess at their names, were greeting each other with loudly exuberant shouts, giving each other fancy left-handed handshakes, embracing with much slapping of backs. There would be no opportunity now of standing at the doors after coming in. People like those two Westerners, the one with the shirt open down to the navel and the other wearing that big straw hat – really was that correct at a party? – would push anybody trying to stand there right out of the way.

It was certainly altogether a very Western occasion. Now that he thought about it, he had hardly heard a single word not in English from any of the people going past or beginning now to fill the alcove behind him. Above the clamour there had risen time and again loud cries of 'Darling' and 'Darling, how lovely'. And there had been public kissing.

A bearer with a freshly loaded tray of snacks, wafting a tongue-tingling odour, was working his way round on a path that would bring him within striking distance at any minute.

He salivated.

And then a sudden great movement through almost the whole of the loudly talking, self-intent gathering caught him up. It was like a sharp gust of wind sending uniform ripples all over the wide surface of a huge lake. Heads turned, voices dropped, there was even something like a single concerted gasp. He followed the direction of it all, to the wide double entrance doors.

There, in a space which had in a few instants somehow cleared itself, stood the two great ones of the *filmi duniya*. Ravi Kumar had arrived escorting Nilima.

Photograph bulbs broke and flashed. Here and there some of the more naïve of the gossip writers actually took notepads from their pockets and began to scribble. As one, the whole assembly turned to each other and spoke.

He has come with her.

She has come with him.

They have come together.

What exactly was said it was impossible to hear. But the meaning was clear enough. Two giant astral bodies had entered temporarily into the same orbit. What it portended, if anything, none could tell. But that it mysteriously affected every single soul in this fragile world was plain beyond doubt. And had to be acknowledged in mere exchanged statements of the facts.

He has come with her.

She has come with him.

They have come with each other.

It was a tribute to the superstars from all the galaxies that swung and glittered beneath them.

Ghote, like all the others round him, looked and looked for the minute or two – it can hardly have been longer – that there was a space round the newcomers. Ravi Kumar was standing, eyes directed to some far, far point, carriage proud, profile clear-cut and poised to conquer. He wore a sportingly cut orangey-buff suit seemingly designed to set off a shirt of the most dazzling peacock blue, in itself created to be no more than a background for the most vibrant psychedelic tie Ghote had ever seen. Only vaguely did the superstar seem aware of Nilima beside him, although her arm was lightly linked in his.

But, to Ghote, Nilima was the sight to feast on. If she had seemed a figure of goddess-like opulence when she had summoned him to her at Talkiestan Studios, she now looked a dozen times more marvellously glamorous. He felt overwhelmingly that the combined imaginations of every ever-dreaming man in all Bombay could not have conjured up the vision that she was.

She wore a sari. A green sari. But it put such a green silk affair as Miss Officewalla had on into the category of a garment stitched out of wilting leaves. Gold threaded it and underlay it and stiffened it and shimmered it. And its own green was so dark and lustrous that it would not have needed even a particle of gold to enhance its beauty and its glow. And Nilima wore it, so it seemed to him standing there at this distance, mouth falling open in mere admiration, as no sari had ever before been worn in the whole history of the world. It clung to her. It embraced her. It hid and revealed her. It promised and it forbade. It was everything. It was all that could possibly be needed.

But there was jewellery also.

Gold lay thick in her hair. Gold cascaded from her ears. Gold lay on her neck, thick, rich and softly giving out its unchangeable message. Gold for a golden one. The earth's most precious ore fit tribute to the earth's most precious person. A goddess. More than a goddess.

The thoughts moved in slow procession through his head in the brief period before renewed movement in the dense crowd blotted out his view. And to think that he himself had talked to that goddess. That it had been only yesterday that she had sat within a yard of him. His fingers had nearly touched hers. He had felt that tiny heat coming from the tips of hers to the tips of his.

And into that world she daily inhabited he might himself gain entrance. He had only to solve this case. That was all. Simply to find the murderer of Dhartiraj, her friend and co-artiste, and he would be welcome in the circle in which she moved. She had asked him to do that, for her. And the means to do it was within his grasp. Only let Jagdish Rana come here tonight, only let him not have fled but be at this moment on his way to flaunt himself at this party and he would have him.

The bearer with the tray of succulent, lightly steaming snacks came and stood right in front of him. A dumpy woman guest was inquiring from him with sharp anxiety whether the contents of the little crispness-covered rolls were truly vegetarian.

'Yes, madam.'

'You are sure?'

'Yes, madam.'

She took one. Popped it into her little round mouth. Swallowed it in one soft gulp and took another. He could easily help himself now.

But the little brown and yellow rolls on their gay plastic cocktail sticks were as ashes to him. Hunger had left him. Consuming ambition blotted out everything.

Jagdish Rana, where was he?

Chapter 14

Suddenly panic beat up in Ghote's heart. What if the failed star had come creeping into the party while all eyes had been on Nilima and Ravi Kumar? While he himself had been gazing, lost, at the golden star? The fellow could be somewhere in the big room at this moment. The crowd was certainly so thick that he could be going about unobserved. He could perhaps stay here as long as necessary to show himself as being defiantly in circulation and then quickly leave.

But no. Jagdish Rana would not enter in the wake of the truly great ones. He would not permit himself to suffer that eclipse. No, had he been on the point of coming in, he would have quietly gone back downstairs and have waited a little, lurked perhaps in those luxurious lavatories down there with their heavy appointments and almost palace-like air. He would wait until the great wave had rippled into quiet. And then he would make his entrance.

And that might, then, be quite soon now.

Oh, why were there so many chattering, laughing, gesticulating people between him and the doors?

He put one foot on the top of the substantial skirting-board beside him and by hooking his fingers behind a pillar up against the wall he managed to heave himself some nine whole inches higher.

It was uncomfortable. His ankle was appallingly cricked. But he did not have to stay there long.

There was a good clear space in front of the doors now with the party plainly at its peak and bearers beginning to load immense supper dishes on two huge tables nearby – one 'Vegetarian', as a bold black-and-white notice proclaimed, the other 'Non-Veg' – and into this space there stepped, quite unexpectedly for all the length of time that he had waited for him, the failed star.

The fellow had chosen his moment well. His entrance could not have failed to catch some eyes, even though people were beginning to move away from the doors down towards the huge platters of pilaus and lobster curries, of mounded kebabs and dark swimmy vindaloos. But the eyes that turned to see who had entered so late flicked away again almost as swiftly as if some leprous beggar had wheeled or poled his way into the big chandelier-glittering room.

Within two minutes of that dramatic and well-contrived

entry no one at all was within hailing distance of the newcomer.

Ghote saw him square up to the rebuff. He could imagine from the sudden sharp tilt of the head the look of resolution that must have come on to his face and how it would for a minute or so pull taut the pouches that sagged under the eyes. He felt a dart of admiration for the fellow's courage. He himself, he suspected, would have turned tail and have crept out meeting with such hostility. But Jagdish Rana was braving them all, thrusting into the crowd now determined to be talked to.

But the fellow was nevertheless his prey. The man he intended to see in the dock on a charge of murder. The murder of a star.

He moved off into the crowd himself. No point in leaving the fellow to find someone at last to greet him or to meet with further rebuffs. His courage might break after all and he might make a bolt for it. The sooner that *Mr Rana, I would like a word, if you please* was spoken the better.

But it was not at all easy to approach him. Down from that uneasy perch at the corner of the alcove, he could no longer see his quarry and the tide of people going towards the supper tables was flowing strongly now so that he was all the time having to push his way through.

'Excuse me.'

'I beg your pardon.'

'Excuse, madam.'

'Sorry, sir.'

He was making infuriatingly slow progress, and leaving a small trail of resentment behind him. But Jagdish Rana must be somewhere at the other end of the room. And that would be all too near the entrance doors.

And that man was his passport to the world above awaiting him. Nilima's golden world.

He thrust and pushed at the noisily talking guests streaming down towards the supper tables.

A bearer came up and offered him a large plate and a napkin-wrapped fork. No fingers-eating here.

He curtly waved him aside.

Then a notion flashed up.

He darted forward and caught him by the elbow.

'Sahib?'

'I am needing the toilet, quickly.'

He hardly had to contrive a look of acute anxiety.

And the idea worked.

'This way, sahib. Follow me.'

The fellow had absolutely mastered the knack of threading through the press. The slow buffeting progress of a minute earlier was transformed behind that white-jacketed back into the easiest of sliding motions. Sometimes they seemed to be going sideways. Once even they actually went back towards the supper. But all the time the end of the big room grew nearer and nearer.

And then there was Jagdish Rana.

He was standing all on his own where the crowd had thinned, a half-empty whisky glass in his hand, quite evidently trying to look like someone pondering over which of his friends to go and talk to next.

But – maddening stroke of ill-luck – he was standing facing exactly in the direction in which he himself and his bearer guide had just emerged from the thicker throng. And the consequence was plain to see on the fellow's face. The sudden look of puzzlement and then the swift dawning of recognition. Recognition, realization and flight.

Ghote experienced a sharp blaze of self-directed rage. If only he had not been so hot in the chase. What had happened to his idea of coming quietly up behind the fellow?

But no time for that now.

Jagdish Rana was walking rapidly away.

Mercifully he was on the other side of the long room from the doors and had a good long way to go to them, but there was almost nobody to block his path.

'Mr Rana,' he called out, loudly as he dared.

It was worth a try. But, as he had really expected, it had exactly the opposite effect from what had been intended. Jagdish Rana simply quickened his pace.

At something not far short of a run, though still decorously enough not to draw attention, he set off to get to the doors first if he could.

Should he actually run? He felt that it would be really very wrong. And, besides, there was a fair chance that he could cut him off.

But then he saw what Jagdish Rana must have already noticed and what had kept him a little unaccountably on the inner side of the room. Behind a wide white-clothed table on which trays of snacks had earlier been put for the bearers to take up there was an unobtrusive door. Unmarked and in the same pale green colour as the big room's walls, it must lead to a service staircase of some sort.

And Jagdish Rana now had only to slip round the end of the wide table to reach it. And beyond it there might well be three or four different escape routes.

He had broken into an undisguised run before he had had time to think. But the sound of his feet thudding on the polished floor must have alerted the escaping star, because he too sprinted a few yards and now had almost reached the service door, his right hand held in front of him to bang it open.

Running full out, Ghote decided in a single instant what he had to do. Hardly decided, rather simply acted.

He dived forward, slid a yard or two across the floor as if on ice and zoomed under the wide white-clothed table.

He felt the heavy damask cloth brush across his head and shoulders. Under the table, it was for one instant cavernously dark. Then he was out, paddling himself with his hands up into a crouch.

And colliding with Jagdish Rana at the opened service door.

He wrapped his arms firmly round but the fellow fought back like a tiger and, anxious to make as little noise as possible, it was all he could do to hold on.

At one point the heaving, jerking star contrived to bang the heel of his shoe hard on to his shin and he let out an involuntary yelp. From the corner of his eye, as he wrestled, he saw faces turning towards them and two or three bearers cautiously approaching.

But in his time he had dealt with too many unwilling arrestees not to know how to tackle them, and it was less than two minutes before he had Jagdish Rana neatly held in front of him, one arm twisted securely and even a little viciously behind his back.

He pushed him hastily through the doorway in which they had fought and found, as he had expected, that there were service stairs leading down. In a very short time he had emerged into the guests' area of the hotel again and was marching his captive without ceremony across the gleaming white foyer, conscious of the raised, interested eyes of the visitors and guests always to be found there and of the efforts of his friend the hotel security officer to interpose his tall frame between them and the inadmissible sight of the sagging-eyed star being hustled out.

Well, he would have to do something some time about putting relations there back on their former good footing. But no. No, he would not need to. Where his life was going at this very moment he would soon be beyond the need to maintain friendly relations with hotel security officers.

The tall glass doors swung open before him as he pushed Jagdish Rana through.

'My vehicle,' he snapped to the magnificently turbanned white-uniformed chaprassi on duty, giving him its number.

The car came up with satisfying promptness at the chaprassi's loudhailer call. He pushed Jagdish Rana in at the back and slid in after him. There was no need to give an order. No sooner had the chaprassi slammed the door closed behind him than they were off.

Sitting in grim silence beside his captive, he allowed himself to jump ahead to the point where he would have him on the other side of his desk at Headquarters and, preliminaries over, they would be getting down to the meat of it. He would teach the fellow to send him on a fool's errand. He would make him pay for every minute spent hunting for Sudhaker Wani, questioning him and finding in the end that he had been negotiating over buying his film song at the time Dhartiraj had been killed. Yes, he would pay.

He would pay by having his real motive for killing Dhartiraj ripped out of him like the inside rottenness of some animal being torn out by some filthy butcher. And he would be made to confess. To confess with every possible detail of circumstances so that the evidence when it came to court would be beyond any doubting. And then, when sentence had been pronounced, there would follow his own golden hour as the day the night.

Seen across his desk, there was no doubt that Jagdish Rana, once the first choice of every producer as Villain till the up-and-coming Dhartiraj had displaced him, was a man in a corner. The eyes showed it, flicking whitely from side to side. The face showed it, blotchily patched with sweat. The very smell of him, the sweat mingling with the sharp noxious odour of a stomach rebelling in acid-swamped fear, showed it to the hilt.

'We are meeting now in altogether different circumstances,' Ghote banged out at him.

He offered no reply.

But it was plain from the sudden quick biting of the lips that he too was recalling their former encounter and how he had planted his dart of suspicion and sent that big absurd circular bed spinning round in his triumph. Was seeing that moment and contrasting it with his situation now, hauled out of a big *filmi* party and bundled up here like the lowest of pickpockets or pimps.

Ghote decided to rub it in.

'We meet in different circumstances. Isn't it?'

Still no answer.

'Speak up, man. Speak up. You are under interrogation now. We meet in different circumstances from the last time you answered my questions. Yes?'

'If you say.'

An ungracious mutter.

'Under what different circumstances, Mr Rana? Under what change of circumstances exactly?'

No reply.

Ghote bounced forward in his chair in simulated rage.

'Because you brought me here,' Jagdish Rana jerked out.

'Yes, brought you here after you had tried to run away. Well, why did you run, Mr Rana? Can you tell me that? Why did you run when I called that I wanted one word only?'

'I did not run. I was leaving. It was a pretty rotten party.'

Ghote produced a good hollow laugh, leaning back in his chair.

'Such a rotten party that you were leaving by servants' entrance? And as fast as you could go? Not the way for a star to behave, Mr Jagdish Rana.'

'I remember. I felt ill. Yes, that was it. How do you know that I was not feeling ill?'

'Oh but yes, Mr Rana. I am sure that you were feeling ill. Very ill. At the sight of a police officer.'

This was easy. It was a pleasure. To play with the fellow like this till the moment came to plunge in the hook and drag the stinking truth to light. And the truth this time it would be. The end of the investigation was in sight. It had gone astonishingly well, but there were times when things did go right. And this case, his biggest by far, for all that at the start it had frightened him as a child is frightened by distant thunder, had really gone wonderfully. He had had his bad moments. He had gone off on the wrong track. But that was almost all the fault of this rat sitting here in front of him. And, that small error dealt with, things could not have gone better. And they would go on going well, right up to the trial and the verdict.

'Oh yes, Mr Rana. Anybody would feel ill at the sight of a police officer when they had on their conscience a murder.'

Now. This was it. Now rip it out.

'But – But, Inspector, you are making a very great mistake.'

'Oh no. Before I was making a mistake. When you did your level best to make sure that I would. Before I was wasting time chasing here, there and everywhere after an individual known by the name of Sudhaker Wani. But now I am not making any mistake at all.'

'But, Inspector, if you were not able to pin anything on that fellow, is it my fault? Inspector, I told you only a few facts that were altogether self-evident.'

'Oh yes, Mr Rana? And what was it you were telling? Exactly how the murder was committed, isn't it? Exactly how the murderer saw the Five-K hanging in the darkness over Dhartiraj's head like a sword. How he caught hold of that dagger. How he went climbing up that ladder. And how, cut, cut, he sliced through the ropes that held that light. So tell me, Mr Rana, how did you know so exactly, exactly how that murder was done? How? Eh? How? How? How?'

And it looked as if he had got there. The face in front of him with its pouchy eyes and that pencil-thin moustache had gone greyer and greyer as each item of his catalogue had smacked into him. Step by step greyer and greyer. Step by step an admission of guilt.

'But, Inspector, it was – Inspector, believe me, I do not know.'

'But I know, Mr Rana. And I know, too, that for the time of the murder you had no alibi whatsoever, that you tried to put one together and altogether miserably failed. So, come, what have you to say now?'

Would it be now, the moment? Now that the words he had pushed and struggled and fought to get at would fall to him like a big succulence-packed jack-fruit falling from its stalk close up to the trunk of the thick tree?

Jagdish Rana's face was dripping with sweat. The smell of his foul breath was strong in the air.

'Inspector, I admit it.'

Hah.

'Inspector, I admit I did not have any alibi. And I agree I told you as if I had been there just how the murder was done. But, Inspector, I had to do that. I had to make you believe that someone else had killed Dhartiraj.'

'Oh, of course, you had to make me believe. You had to make me believe anything rather than that you were the murderer. But do you think I am a fool only? Do you think they would be putting someone who was a blithering idiot on to the Dhartiraj case? Oh no. And, though your damn lies may have put me on the wrong track for a few hours, by God, in the end I –'

'Inspector.'

The failed star's voice rang out with desperation.

'Inspector, it was not me. It was not me, I tell you. But how could I have told you then what I knew? How could I be the person to have to tell? I am no more a great favourite of the fans, I admit, but what if I had been the one to betray that, unknown to all, who had gone slinking into Talkiestan Studios by climbing the back wall just at the time of the murder but Ravi Kumar himself?'

Chapter 15

A sense of sky-wide awe filled Ghote's mind. Ravi Kumar. Ravi Kumar, the unchallenged superstar, the man watched by millions all over India from the towering slopes of the mighty Himalayas to the distant southern-most tip of the sub-continent, and beyond, too, as far as Hindi films ever went, to England, to the Arab world, to Turkey, to Africa, to Russia. Ravi Kumar had been given him as the true murderer of Dhartiraj, the man who had motive enough in having lost his mistress to the popular player of Villains and who now, contrary to every belief, had been seen within a few yards of the place where the murder had happened at the very time of the crime. Ravi Kumar. It was as if the President of the United States of America had been shown up as the killer in some squalid quarrel over a woman of the streets of the British Foreign Secretary. It was as if one god had stuck a knife into another, and he himself, a humble serving police officer, had to make the arrest.

How plain now were the reasons for Jagdish Rana's wrigglings and writhings. Easy to see now how the fellow would have done almost anything, told any lies, pointed to any other possible suspect, to avoid this appalling betrayal and the total sentence of banishment from society that would follow. To be the man who had denounced Ravi Kumar, it was worse than being the man who would have to arrest him.

No. As bad. As bad as being the officer who should have to carry out the arrest of Ravi Kumar. And that was himself, Ganesh Ghote.

He sat in utter silence. Opposite him Jagdish Rana sat equally without making the least sound. Only the lingering odour of his stomach-ravaged breath – no wonder that he had been in such acute internal distress – hung in the trapped air.

For long, long seconds there was room for nothing else in Ghote's mind but the stupendous fact he had learnt. But at last, and still without a single word or even a sound being uttered, a new feeling began slowly to grow up inside him.

It was a thought of such daring that at first he could not credit his own head with having formed it. But little by little it took root and grew and flowered with at last an abundance of blossom. It was the thought that, if Ravi Kumar had to be arrested, then there was after all a man fit for the task. If the superstar had to be led away to a common cell, then Inspector Ganesh Ghote was, strange though it seemed, the man to do it.

He had been chosen. Inconceivable as the idea had been once, he could accept it now. For the superstar there had to be a super-detective and he was that person.

And no sooner had he, in all but actual fact, spoken aloud that immense thought than his mind, as if released from an obliterating weight, began to work in lightning jumps of activity. If Ravi Kumar was to be charged with the murder of Dhartiraj, the facts of the matter must be discovered and collated. If, before, he had been determined to present a foolproof, a lawyer-proof, case against Jagdish Rana, how much more necessary it would be to assemble a perfect case against Ravi Kumar, the man all India would demand to see freed.

So every fact of what the superstar had done would have to be brought to light. But in doing that – he saw in an instantly lucid flash – he would have to act with the greatest caution. No one – not even a super-sleuth – could go about asking questions, checking alibis, making observations, taking measurements which would be seen as incriminating a figure of such magnitude until the time had come to make the arrest. No, he must proceed testing each step, one at a time.

'You saw Ravi Kumar inside the Studios at the time Dhartiraj died?' he abruptly asked the failed star sitting in front of him.

The breaking of the silence in his little office seemed even to him an outrage. There should have followed after Jagdish Rana's accusing words a hushed silence lasting hour upon hour. And could it be no more than half a minute since he had heard them?

'Yes,' the failed star answered, as if he too felt the desecration. 'Yes, Inspector, I saw him.'

'And where exactly was it that you saw?'

Keep it calm. Just as if it was any ordinary interrogation.

'Inspector, it was over the back wall that I saw him climb.'

'The back wall? There is a way of entering the Studios compound there? Where exactly is this?'

'Inspector, I could show you the place. There is a narrow space between the wall of Sound Stage No. 2 and the end of the Property Department. Often they leave properties there that are too big to be stored inside. And a few weeks ago they put, right up against the compound wall, the keys from a giant typewriter they had used in a dance sequence when they had one girl on each key. They are piled one against the other and they make it possible to come down from the top of the wall – it is about fifteen feet high, you know – as if by a sort of big staircase. On the other side, you see, there is a banyan tree growing quite close to the wall.'

'And how was it that you came to be there yourself?'

'Because when I am working at Talkiestan that is where I leave my car.'

A swift bitter smile appeared under the knife-edge of his moustache.

'There was a time,' he added, 'when I could leave it right in the front, under the big gul mohar tree.'

'But now you leave it at the back in such a position that you can see the gap between Sound Stage No. 2 and the Property Department?'

'Yes. And I was sitting in the car learning my dialogues when he came over the wall. I noticed first when he was cutting the wire at the top.'

'Cutting the wire?'

'Yes, there is an extra fence on top of the wall there because otherwise it would be possible to get over by climbing the banyan. You sometimes see boys up there, looking in. And I noticed a man there with wire-cutters. I was going to call some security fellows. But then I recognized Ravi Kumar.'

So the superstar had gone to so much trouble to get into the Studios unobserved. There could hardly be any doubt left about why he had done so.

'You recognized?' he asked, feeling the weight of the burden grow and blowing up his determination to shoulder it.

'Yes, I recognized even though he was wearing a headcloth pulled low so that the end covered almost all his face. I could not at first believe what I had seen. Ravi Kumar never wears any sort of a hat so that he can always be recognized by the fans.'

'But you knew who it was?'

'Well, yes, Inspector. It was something in the way that he jumped down from the wall on to the top of one of the big typewriter keys. Otherwise I would not. He was wearing a long old white shirt as well, with its tails down to his knees almost. Ravi Kumar who is the smartest dresser in the whole film community.'

Ghote felt he could see exactly the man who had jumped down so lithely from the high saddle of the old sports car to rebuke his director at Nataraj Studios.

'Why was it that you did not speak with him?' he asked.

'Inspector, almost I did. Almost I came out of my car and made a joke with him. Until I remembered.'

'You remembered? What did you remember?'

'That I was no longer making jokes with Ravi Kumar. That he would no longer speak with someone who soon was not at all going to be in the same circle.'

The fading star spoke with such simple bitterness that for the first time Ghote felt pity for him. To have been in that golden world and to know that its doors were slowly closing against you for ever.

'So you stayed in your car and you watched him?' he asked.

'Yes. I had the glass up on the side which faced outwards so that people would not see me there, and so I was able to watch him.'

135

'And what did he do?'

'He walked up to the corner and then he looked out. And, when he saw that there was nobody near, he darted.'

'He darted? Where?'

'Into Sound Stage No. 2, Inspector. And after ten minutes only he came out and left by the way he had come. And quite soon after that people came running everywhere to say that Dhartiraj was dead.'

'I see.'

One thing Ghote could do to check Jagdish Rana's story without giving anyone an idea that he suspected none other than Ravi Kumar of having murdered Dhartiraj. And that was to go and have a good look at the place where the failed star had said that Ravi Kumar had got over the Talkiestan Studios wall. But for this he needed daylight.

So at the late hour at which he finished questioning Jagdish Rana all that he was able to do was to have him taken back to his home and order a guard to be kept on him. It was not that he suspected that what he had been told had been another attempt to send him off on a false trail. There had been altogether too much anguish in the telling for that to be possible. But, when it came to the trial, Jagdish Rana, willing or not, was going to be one of his principal witnesses.

But, that done, he found he could not at all face going home to get a few hours' sleep. The small routines and circumstances of home life seemed insupportable with all the mountain-looming heights so close in front of him. Everything that until now had been comforting, the small size of the rooms, the familiar smell, taste and consistency of the food his Protima cooked for him, even the awkward heavy dribble in the spray of the shower that always struck just at the same spot on the left-hand side of his head, seemed suddenly intolerably confining and mean.

He decided 'to doze it' on a bench just outside the office, as he had done on numerous other occasions when a case had kept him most of the night.

But he was up and awake well before dawn, standing under a shower that was much less comfortable than his own at home,

136

despite its dribble, getting himself a shave that, for all the expert hands of the barber, was plainly more sore than his own work with his own razor, drinking a single cup of tea and not enjoying it.

At last, however, it was nearly light enough to start on his examination of the Studios' compound wall.

He drove himself, guarding against the least possibility of what he was doing coming to any ears that might draw the correct conclusion. And as he went through the almost traffic-free streets, just springing to view with the coming of the light, excitement began to stir in him at the thought of what the next half-hour might bring. The everyday early morning sights, people emerging bent double from pavement shacks and making their way to the roadside taps, vendors beginning to arrange their goods, oranges or padlocks or pairs of socks, in elaborate piles, a man sitting up suddenly from his spread-out sleeping mat, getting to his feet and rolling up the mat all in almost one movement – each passed in front of his eyes like a cinema film flicking its grey images on to the screen while real events went on elsewhere.

In a few minutes he was at the Talkiestan gates, still closed and silent at this early hour. But he paid them no attention and instead drove carefully all round the outside of the big compound until he came to the long narrow street that ran parallel to the high back wall.

Here he abandoned his car just in the entrance to a lane and set out cautiously on foot.

People were waking into life in this back-street area, too. A taxi-driver had begun to give his vehicle a careful wash. A solitary youth on a bicycle made his way along the middle of the empty street, weaving this way and that as if still half-asleep. From the far end, where there was, he remembered, a mosque, there came the high pleading sound of the muezzin's call.

It did not take long to find the banyan tree whose branches overhung the compound wall. It grew at the end of a short and very narrow lane formed by the fact that the two buildings on either side, a small blue-painted temple and an establishment called the Moon Winding Works, a business specializing in re-winding burnt-out electric motors, did not butt up against each other, perhaps to allow access to the holy banyan.

The little lane – it was hardly wider than four feet – had, however, also plainly found another use. To judge from the stink, it formed a convenient public lavatory and was also used as an unofficial rubbish-dump.

Ghote made his way over two or three squelchy mounds of discarded paper and rags, sending a scrawny chicken squawking and flapping out of the way, and came up to the tree whose long brown dangling ropelike roots fell to the surface of the lane itself, on to the roof of the Moon Winding Works and down inside the high blue temple wall.

It was easy to see how anybody with some agility – and Ravi Kumar certainly had that – could have swung himself up by those thick roots into the body of the tree and from there on to the top of the high Studios' wall. And up on the wall the sprung-back lengths of barbed wire, plainly freshly cut, provided final evidence that Jagdish Rana had been describing something that had actually taken place.

Standing back at the corner of the Moon Winding Works, leaning against the cupboard-like stall of a cigarette vendor, its doors fastened for the night by a cheap padlock, Ghote gave himself to considering exactly what must have taken place at this spot shortly before, in the Studios on the other side of the high wall at the end of the lane, Dhartiraj had died.

There was nobody very much about at this moment, though at that later hour of the morning there would have been at least a few people passing by. A car would have driven up and have been parked, perhaps just inside the very lane opposite, where his own vehicle was. It would certainly not have been Ravi Kumar's ivory-coloured Mercedes, the one he had seen on his visit to the Nataraj Studios. It would have been instead some other deliberately chosen nondescript car, an old Ambassador probably, the like of thousands and thousands on the Bombay streets. It would have been borrowed, without asking, from one of the superstar's *chumchas*.

Its solitary occupant, dressed in a common white shirt with

long dangling tails and a headcloth artfully arranged to cover most of his face, would have sat waiting until there was no one at the entrance to the lane. Then he would have slipped out of the car, have hastily locked it, rapidly crossed the narrow street and made his way down to the old banyan at the end of the rubbish-piled lane. One glance back to make sure no one had entered behind him, and then a quick heave upwards and in a few seconds he would be on the wall. Then out with his wire-cutters and to work.

Yes, that was how it must have been.

It would be necessary to check his own recollection of the lie of the land on the far side when the Studios opened for the day, but there could be little doubt of it now. Ravi Kumar had entered the Talkiestan Studios. It would have been a slightly risky thing to have done but not until that dagger was lifted to cut the Five-K's ropes would anyone who had spotted him have had the least idea what it was he was intending to do. And if he had been spotted he could have called the whole thing off. No, it was risky but not too risky. And to commit a murder without taking any risk would be expecting altogether too much of life, even for a superstar.

So now there was only one thing to do. To confront Ravi Kumar, superstar, with the reality of the deed he had done.

Chapter 16

Ghote found the superstar at his home. Not without difficulty.

Asking the encyclopedic Miss Officewalla where he was likely to be had, of course, been out of the question. The least hint that he wanted to see Ravi Kumar might have had a special issue of *Film Femme* on the streets with the words blazoned across its cover 'CID Accuses Ravi'.

So he had had to find his way through the *filmi* jungle on his own. It had not been easy. On the telephone he met from film studios and film companies a series of rebuffs. *Is Mr Ravi Kumar working there today? Who is that calling, if you please?* And that was a question he dared not answer. He was tempted many times to say that Inspector Ghote of Crime Branch CID urgently wanted to interview Mr Kumar. It would come to that in the end, he felt almost certain. But not so utterly certain that he could afford to have the whole world know the gigantic fact that a superstar was to be accused of murder.

It was only when, in mere desperation, he simply looked up Ravi Kumar in the telephone directory – it was like finding one of the gods listed among a whole column of simple Mr Khrishnas or as one of any number of businesses styled Lakshmi – and rang his house that he began to get anywhere.

Yes, someone had answered, Ravi Kumar is at home. He was going to Talkiestan for the morning shift but he had not left yet.

He looked at his watch.

'But it is already ten o'clock,' he said. 'Isn't it that the morning shift begins at eight ack emma?'

'Ravi Kumar does not get to the Studios before eleven,' came the lofty response.

At that he banged down the receiver and hurried to his car.

But, up at the big house on Pali Hill, looking down from the sea-jutting promontory on to half the teeming insect world of Bombay, he met with a whole new bristling crop of difficulties. He had seen himself arriving, ringing at a bell beside a gate – a superstar would have to ensure himself privacy – handing in a letter saying that 'Inspector G. V. Ghote, CID wishes to see Mr Ravi Kumar in connection with the unfortunate event at the Talkiesan Studios' and very soon after that being respectfully shown to see a cautiously apprehensive superstar.

But things did not at all turn out like that. True, there was a gate, ornate, filling every inch of the archway in the high white wall that surrounded the property and firmly locked. And there was a bell. And, when he had thrust his way through the small group of onlookers waiting to catch a possible glimpse of their hero and had rung at it, a chowkidar did appear, eventually.

He handed him his letter, which he had taken the precaution of making sure was thoroughly sealed, but the man, a surly-looking individual in a dull red cotton uniform, simply took it and tossed it, in full view of all the watchers, on to a bench just inside the gate on which there were already lying a dozen other letters, mostly looking very grubby, and three or four small parcels tied with many windings of fine cotton string.

This was something he would not stand for. Damn it, he might end this visit by taking away the fellow's master under arrest.

He called him back.

There was no answer.

He put his finger on the bell push and kept it there. In a minute or so the fellow reappeared.

'Go away or I will be calling the police,' he shouted.

'I am the police.'

The fellow laughed.

Ghote felt rage compacting itself inside him. Oh, to yell back that not only was he the police but that he was the one policeman ready to arrest superstar Ravi Kumar. But the time was not yet. Not just yet.

Bitterly he dug into his pocket and brought his hand out clutching an impressive handful of notes.

'That letter is Number One urgent priority,' he said.

The chowkidar put a broken-nailed hand through a gap in the ironwork of the gate and took the money.

'No. 1 priority, *jee* sahib,' he said insolently.

But he did take away the letter.

And before very long he came back once more, hauled a long key from the pocket of his red uniform, put it in the lock of the gates and opened them just wide enough for someone to slip through, provided they were prepared to turn a little sideways, and beckoned to Ghote.

Ghote, despite his stoked-up inner knowledge, was prepared to turn a little sideways.

Inside, the chowkidar pointed to the door of a large white-painted house across a garden as big as a small public park and Ghote set off.

He walked slowly, going over in his mind the interview ahead. But he could not help noticing the garden: it showed so many signs of extraordinarily lavish care. Not only was every patch of grass finely mown and miraculously green but the

141

whole area had been worked at till there was room for nothing more. There were raised flower-beds and there were sunken ones, and each was not only brilliant with flowers but its earth was teased into the merest granules. There were walls by the dozen, running here and there, and there were ponds and fountains. And on every available surface there stood a statue. The whole world appeared to have been ransacked to provide them. Not only were all the Hindu gods there, and many more than once, but there were Buddhas by the dozen and whole regiments of little European figures, funny little men in bright red conical hats with tiny grinning faces engaged in such occupations as fishing and raking. Enormous sums of money must have been spent on the place. But no doubt that was the object.

At the house itself there was another bell to be rung. It came in the centre of a formidable wooden door studded all over with large black bolt-heads. After a shorter wait than at the gate it was opened by a bearer attired in a white uniform with a full magnificent red turban and broad red cummerbund.

Ghote felt he was getting near the heart of it all.

'Mr Ravi Kumar is expecting me,' he said sharply. 'I have sent a letter.'

Without a word the bearer ushered him into a spacious hall, its floor flagged with black-and-white marble, its walls hung with the superstar's innumerable trophies of fame. Through an open doorway Ghote glimpsed the dark interior of a projection theatre.

Well, this was it. The superstar's home. His citadel. And the invader had entered it.

He made himself taller.

The bearer showed him into a room that he supposed was the dining-room and left him, still in silence. There was a long table glinting with so much polish that it looked like a pool of still water. Drawn up to it were a dozen upright chairs with ornately carved backs painted a glossy white and seats of deep red velvet, very highly sprung. They would not, he thought, be pleasant to sit on if the air-conditioning was not working at full blast. In the middle of the table there were four many-branched silver candle-holders, the tall twisty red candles in them almost matching in colour the velvet of the chairs. On the walls were similar candle-holders, though these had dummy candles with little electric light bulbs in them.

Something about the candles on the table caught Ghote's eye and he peered forward and inspected them. They showed no sign of use, their wicks were white and they were covered in a faint layer of dust.

Not surprising, he thought. The heat from them all would be intolerable.

But after this discovery he found nothing more to do. He went over in his mind once or twice more what he hoped to learn from Ravi Kumar, but there was nothing else to be done there. He peered through the slats of the window blinds at the enormous garden and watched the shadow of a cloud slowly pass across it.

The minutes went by.

It was inadmissible to keep a police officer working on a case of this importance waiting like this.

He went to the door and peered out. The big black-and-white flagged hall was still and empty.

What if his letter had alerted the superstar? Was he at this instant making his way by fast car out to Santa Cruz to take a plane to Europe or America? Or, more likely, was he busy arranging himself at huge cost some unbreakable alibi?

He was on the point of marching out, going into whatever rooms presented themselves, shouting and demanding till he located the superstar, when he heard the slap of bare feet coming from a corridor at the far end of the hall. Hastily he stepped back inside the dining-room and pulled its door quietly closed.

A few moments later the door was opened again. An old servant stood there, barefoot, gnarled of face, almost black of skin.

Ghote guessed at once that this must be Ravi Kumar's personal servant. No one else would have dared to be dressed the way he was in a baggy pyjama with an old shirt at the top, its long tails dangling down.

And that shirt. He knew, strongly as if he had seen it all with his own eyes, that this had been the very garment that the superstar had worn when he had climbed into the Talkiestan Studios. There would have been not the slightest difficulty in borrowing it off this fellow's back. And it would be next to impossible ever to gain an admission that this had happened. The fellow would, in all probability, have been Ravi Kumar's servant even before his film days. Someone bound to him and his family before him. And his confidant now, sometimes disapproving, but hearing everything and never, ever, telling anything.

'Come,' the man said.

Ghote followed him, out into the trophy-hung hall, round the corner and along a wide corridor. He went over, for one last time, the way he meant the interview ahead to go.

It would be tricky. There was no denying that. For all that it looked certain that the superstar had disguised himself and entered the Talkiestan Studios in secret just before Dhartiraj had been done to death, the case was not yet proven. And, if by some extraordinary chance the supposition he had made turned out to be wrong, then to have accused a figure as colossally influential as Ravi Kumar of a crime as terrible as killing a fellow star, why, it would be worse than suicide. But if, on the other hand, he really was on the point of coming face to face with the man who had cut loose that Five-K light to fall on the hapless star below, then he had to tread even more carefully. What he had to do was to get the superstar to betray himself. To say something that he should not have known, could not have known. That would give him the final conclusive proof that the extraordinary task that seemed to have fallen to him was indeed what it appeared. And then he could act.

But he must not put his opponent on his guard.

The long-shirted servant pattering along in front of him had swept open the door at the end of the corridor and was standing aside for him to go in. This was it.

'It is Ghote sahib.'

He registered that the superstar had apparently not told even this confidential servant that his visitor was a CID inspector. Then his eyes took in the huge room in front of him.

Huge though it was, it was apparently the superstar's bedroom and it reduced to mere nothingness that other luxury *filmi* bedroom he had seen, the one with the absurd turntable bed where he had first interviewed Jagdish Rana out at Juhu. The bed here was on a scale as big as the room and the superstar lay in it flopped on a heap of fifteen or twenty pillows, each covered in a smart chocolate-brown striped material matching the sheets. Spread here and there over the deeply-valanced gold-threaded bedcover were newspapers, carelessly discarded, almost a dozen different magazines, a scatter of glossy photographs, a transistor radio, many-knobbed and playing *filmi* music, a big hand-mirror in the shape of a lotus leaf, two different trays with cups and plates on them, and heaps of letters, opened and unopened.

He looked for his own among them. But, though its official buff envelope would have stood out among all the ones he saw, he was unable to spot it. Was it somewhere hidden among all those stripey pillows?

He stepped forward.

Ravi Kumar was regarding him carelessly. Or was he? The nearer he got the more it looked as though the superstar's gaze was directed not at him but at perhaps a crowd somewhere in the distance behind him.

Almost he turned to make sure there was not a small group standing admiringly in the doorway he had left.

He crossed the soft carpet, glancing a little this way and that at the huge mirror-hung room. Beyond its windows, out on a veranda, he saw there were four or five men lounging in wicker armchairs, reading magazines and playing cards. The superstar's *chumchas*, no doubt. Well, with the noise of that transistor they would hardly be able to hear that the two of them were talking at all, let alone what was being said.

But even when he got right up to the bed the superstar was still looking loftily at that imaginary crowd in the doorway.

He cleared his throat, noisily as he could.

Ravi Kumar seemed not to have heard. But perhaps the unceasing flow of honey-sweet music from the transistor was to blame.

He tried again. A whole consumptives' chorus of phlegm-rattling.

And this time the superstar did at least raise an inquiring eyebrow.

Well, that would have to be enough introduction. The man knew who he was, and he knew who it was in in front of him. His opponent. Then get ready for battle.

'Mr Kumar, I have come to ask you when it was that you last saw the late Dhartiraj?'

For second after second the superstar did not reply. He lay back on his great mound of striped pillows with the many-knobbed transistor pouring out its honey-music somewhere by his knees and he looked into that far distance where a crowd was adulating him.

But under a steady gaze he proved unable to keep the pose up indefinitely, and abruptly he reached forward, picked up the first magazine that came to hand and started to read. It was *Star and Style* and there was a picture of himself in colour on the page where it had been open.

But the gesture was all Ghote needed.

'Mr Kumar, when?' he jabbed out.

'How should I know?' the superstar answered with give-away promptness. 'Yes, certainly I would talk with Dhartiraj. But it is a well-known fact that he and I were not friends. I probably saw him last at some party or other.'

'You did not see him shortly before his death? Where were you that morning, Mr Kumar?'

And the look in his eyes then was almost enough. They showed a quick but unmistakable glint of a buried fear being unsettlingly confirmed.

It was almost enough. But not quite. He felt he had to have words to back it up. Words that could eventually be incorporated in a report. *In answer to the question Witness said . . .*

But Witness said nothing that helped.

'Inspector, I refuse to answer all these ridiculous questions.'

And he heaved himself off his pillow mound, leant forward with effort and, twisting one of the transistor's many knobs,

146

made the outpouring of music that had surrounded them twice as loud as it had been and more.

There could have been no more effective way of indicating that the interview was at an end.

Chapter 17

For perhaps ten minutes after Ravi Kumar had so brutally obliterated his interrogation with the thick treacle of blaring *filmi* music Ghote tried to continue. Once he began to slide his arm across the rich bedcover towards the almost quivering transistor with the aim of reducing its volume by just a little. But the superstar spotted his manoeuvre long before it was near success and snatched the many-knobbed machine to his chest, where he actually contrived to increase yet more its honey-blare.

Soon after that Ghote gave up. He turned and marched out of the big room.

It came as no surprise to find the superstar's black-skinned draggle-shirted servant standing just outside the door waiting to escort him to the gate.

He left furiously plotting how to overcome the breathtaking opposition he had met with. He must show he was the man's match. Plainly, though, he would not get to see him again just by asking. He had been lucky to get as far as he had. No doubt the superstar must have decided, probably not without misgivings, to see whether the request for an interview meant that the police were in any way suspicious of him. And then, when he had at last got in to see the man, that single question about where he had been at the time of Dhartiraj's murder had been quite enough.

Driving slowly southwards through the northern suburbs of the city towards Headquarters, lost in these thoughts, he suddenly almost brought the car to a halt.

By golly, if Ravi Kumar had been so alerted by that one question, it added a powerfully strong link to the chain of reasoning that said he was indeed Dhartiraj's murderer. If only there was one more witness to that climb-in at Talkiestan beside Jagdish Rana. It was only too easy to imagine what a clever defence pleader would make of the bitter failed star in the witness-box. *Mr Rana, had you any reason to be jealous of my client, Mr Ravi Kumar?* It would need only that to make his foundations crumble.

If only there had been, inside the compound or outside it, someone about at the time Ravi Kumar had got over that wall. A simple *mochi*, sitting on his haunches at the street corner making a sandal while he waited for some passer-by to offer him a repair. Anything.

But there would not have been. For one simple reason. If there had been anybody there to see, Ravi Kumar would have stayed sitting in his anonymous borrowed car till the coast was clear. The street there was never so busy that there would not be short periods when it would have been possible to slip into the lane between the temple and the Moon Winding Works unobserved.

Yet – he was now jockeying the car round by Opera House: there was a hell of a queue for the morning performance at the cinema, must be a real hit-film – if only, say, that cigarette-vendor with the stall on the corner of the Moon Winding Works had been there. At round about ten in the morning he ought to have been. But he must have left his post for some reason. Ravi Kumar would never have walked right past him into the lane. Perhaps he had gone for a skimpy cup of single tea somewhere, or perhaps he occasionally made use of the services of a doorstep barber nearby. But might he not have been back at his stall when Ravi Kumar crossed over the wall on his way out?

It was a chance. Just a chance. But perhaps a chance worth looking into.

The turning to the left into Charni Road was there. He swung round into it and headed north once more. It was a long way back. But it might, it just might, be worth it.

But getting to the narrow street behind the Talkiestan Studios took exasperatingly long. As always when he was in a hurry, every other driver, not to speak of every other innumerable cyclist and roadway-walking pedestrian, seemed to be bent on frustrating him. And with every fresh hold-up the importance of seeing that cigarette vendor seemed to grow. There was no reason to suppose he would hold a vital clue, but the notion that he did so became minute by minute more firmly fixed in his head.

It was nearly an hour later that he at last turned into the long street behind the Studios.

Though by no means blocked by traffic, it was very much busier than when he had seen it at dawn. Cars, lorries and the occasional yellow-topped taxi, their progress complicated by slow-moving bullock carts, horse-drawn victorias, long heavily-loaded two-wheel pushcarts and bicycles by the score, slowly jostled their way along. On the pavements, where their narrowness and pot-holed state permitted, people were drifting from one dark little shop to another, pausing to look at the arrays of foods or sweetmeats, standing to bargain over a sale or stopping to ponder deeply which number at the lottery-ticket-seller's was likely to be lucky that day.

He halted at the first lane he came to and abandoned the car. It would be quicker on foot.

But again his very haste seemed to create obstacles. He could see over the slowly-moving heads the blue-painted roof of the temple at the corner he was making for. But first a boy, occupying all of one flat area of pavement to lay out his mother's newly-cooked chapatties to cool, hopped right under his feet and nearly sent him sprawling. Then a slightly mad leper, for some inexplicable reason, selected him as his target and would not get out of his path, even when he had given him all the small change he had. Next a pickpocket he knew of old came up and made a performance of claiming his acquaintance. This last delay so irritated him that he began to imagine seeing, down by the blue temple, as totally unlikely a figure of Ravi Kumar's shirt-dangling servant.

But when, battered and bad-tempered, he at last reached the corner of the Moon Winding Works the cigarette-vendor was at last there, the doors of his cupboard-stall open, busy selling two Chaminars from a crumpled packet to a clerk from some nearby office.

He could hardly wait for the transaction to be completed.

'Police,' he said to the vendor, flashing his identity card, as soon as the clerk had turned away.

The man immediately looked panic-stricken. But he was not so much so that he was unable to answer questions.

No, he said simply, three days before at ten in the morning he had not been at his stall. He had gone to the hospital, to get something for his chest.

He coughed prodigiously to show how necessary that had been.

Ghote was turning away, unable to believe his idea had proved fruitless, for all that his reason told him that nothing had been more likely, when the vendor, coughing completed, added something else.

'But, Inspectorji, if you are wanting to know what went on in the lane at that time, you could speak with old Kesar. She is always here in the morning.'

'Old Kesar?'

Hope was spuming up in him again.

'She spends the morning picking over the rags and paper she has gathered,' the vendor explained. 'And it is here that she sleeps also.'

He laughed, and coughed again at length.

'You would be saying she looks like no more than a heap of rags herself,' he said, as soon as he was able. 'Often when she was lying there I have not known until she moved.'

Ghote peered along the narrow lane down towards the dangling roots of the banyan. He could see no one.

'But it is still morning,' he said. 'Where is she?'

If the old rag-picker was really as inconspicuous when she was lying down as the vendor had said, what would be more likely than that Ravi Kumar had walked right past her on his way to climb the tree? And, in a lane so narrow, was it not also more than likely that he would have disturbed her? Enough to have made her look up? And perhaps remember him?

His other witness. At last.

'Inspectorji, she is not here any more.'

'Not here any more? What do you mean? What?'

'Inspector, just ten minutes ago some men came and took.'

'Took? Took? What are you meaning "took"?'

'I was thinking they must be her family, Inspector. But I did not know she had family. I was thinking that they had come at last to take her to hospital. God knows she needs it more than I even. A thousand things she must have wrong with her, old Kesar.'

'But what men? Which way did they go?'

'Inspectorji, I am not knowing. All I am knowing is that first a fellow came looking down the lane till he saw old Kesar. And then he was calling to some more fellows, and they came and they did not say a word but they picked up old Kesar and left, carrying her like a bundle only.'

'The fellow who came first,' Ghote jabbed out, horrible suspicions rapidly confirming themselves in his mind, 'was he a fellow with a long dangling white shirt and a black face, a shirt down to his knees?'

The vendor lifted up his bare skinny arms in open amazement.

'Inspector, it was he.'

'Which way? Why way did he go?'

But the vendor had not seen them after they had turned down the street out of his view. And, although Ghote ran out at once in pursuit, he knew even as he did so that it would be useless. They had had too much of a start, Ravi Kumar's personal servant and the *goondas* he must have hired.

And so it proved. An exhausting jostling run all along the remaining length of the road produced not the least glimpse of any party of men carrying an old rag-picking woman like a bundle. But it would have been all too easy for them to have taken her down some lane to be lost at once among a maze of buildings or to have had some sort of vehicle waiting and to have taken off in that.

Ghote at last came to a halt, panting and with every limb slithery with sweat.

He felt sick, too.

Sick, not so much from exertion, though no doubt running

151

and dodging through the street crowd at full pelt for a good quarter of a mile under the heat of the sun had had some effect on him, but rather sick from ill-success.

Once again he had been thwarted by the superstar. First, that blank defeat in the huge bedroom of the house on Pali Hill. And now, when with a little more quickness of thought and decisiveness of action he could have jumped one step ahead, he had been beaten again. No doubt Ravi Kumar, going over everything he had done in getting into the Studios to cut down that Five-K over Dhartiraj's head in the light of the clear CID interest in his movements, had remembered the old rag-picker he had seen or half-seen in the lane and had decided not to risk her realizing, unlikely though it was, that in her dirt-engrained old hands she held a vital clue against him. And, once he had made that decision, he had acted. With superstar speed.

Ghote, leaning against a battered red black-domed post-box, gave himself to thought.

At least now it was clear beyond any remaining shadow of doubt that Ravi Kumar was his man. The fellow had shown that he had something to hide that was worth taking a considerable risk over. But, this one weakness dealt with, he must now believe himself altogether secure. Up there on his superstar's pinnacle, he must think that he was beyond the reach of the law.

But he would find out differently.

Very well, perhaps he himself as a simple inspector might have some difficulty in reaching to him on his own. But he could be the force that saw that those powerful enough to get to him reached up there and let him pull him down.

If Ravi Kumar was very, very influential, so was the Commissioner of Bombay Police. And so was the Deputy Commissioner in charge of Crime Branch.

The Deputy Commissioner had said that he would have to let it be known he was taking a personal interest in the case. Well, it would be necessary for him to do a little more. To accompany his inspector to that big house up on Pali Hill to effect the arrest.

Yes, by God.

He pushed himself away from the support of the post-box, turned and marched off in the direction of his car.

The Deputy Commissioner agreed to see him without the least delay. Looking into his big office through the square of glass in the door before entering, Ghote could not help recalling the days and the days that had passed with him thinking he was never going to get work of sufficient importance to get his orders direct from here. But now all that was changed. A high fate had all along been reserved for him, and now that it had come he was equal to its claims, to the last one.

He pushed wide the door.

'Ah, Ghote, yes. What can I do for you?'

The words were certainly welcoming. How extraordinary they would have seemed less than a week ago. But somewhere behind them was there a hint of caution? But why should there be?

No, he was imagining things. He must learn to get rid of such phantom suspicions. He was above worrying in that petty way now. He must start behaving with all that unthinking assurance of the stars. Yes, he must behave like a detective star.

He pulled out one of the four chairs lined up with precision in front of the big desk and sat down.

'It is my investigation, sir,' he said. 'It has taken an altogether most serious turn.'

But now there could be no mistaking it. The Deputy Commissioner's face had registered, if only for a moment, dismay. Or more than that: the confirmation of something long feared.

No time now to work out what the look could mean. Just time to note that it had been there and to feel a sudden bottomless disquiet.

'Sir,' he said, suddenly able only to push the words out as best he could. 'Sir, I have proof. Sir, not necessarily a case ready to go to court, sir, but altogether enough to act on. To act on with your assistance, sir. Sir, I shall need that most definitely. It is Mr Ravi Kumar, sir.'

And, yes, on to the Deputy Commissioner's mobile and

quick-darting features there had not come the look of intense astonishment that there ought to have done at those words.

Instead he had pursed his lips in recognition of a plainly expected calamity.

'Yes, Ghote, Ravi Kumar,' he said.

'Sir, in the course of my investigation I questioned a certain film star, or rather a certain ex-film star, a Mr – '

'Ghote.'

'Sir?'

'Ghote, there is no need for you to go over the whole course of your investigation. It is enough for me to know that you have good reason to believe that Ravi Kumar himself killed Dhartiraj. You have good reason?'

'Yes, sir.'

'Then act on it, Inspector. Act on it. It is your simple duty as Investigating Officer in the case.'

'But – But, sir, I think I shall be needing your support, sir. Ravi Kumar is a great star, sir. A superstar and – '

'I do not need you to tell me what Ravi Kumar is, Inspector.'

The Deputy Commissioner was, beyond doubt, irritated. It was something he himself had never heard from him before, nor expected to hear. Angry he could be, on occasion, when anger was justified. But never peevishly irritated. Never.

'Sir,' he ventured nevertheless, 'your assistance and support, sir.'

'Ghote, let me spell it out for you. Almost as soon as I had been informed of the murder of Dhartiraj I received certain other intelligence, vague and doubtful intelligence' – his eyes flicked to the direct-line telephone beside him, and Ghote saw failed Jagdish Rana sitting on that absurd circular bed and tapping with too much pride on the little book of telephone numbers in his shirt pocket – 'but enough to make me realize that what you have discovered in the case was a possibility. I had to consider, then, how the affair should be handled in the light of what might happen. And in due course I decided that what was necessary was an investigation by an officer who would get at the facts – if what I feared turned out to be the facts – but who was sufficiently low-ranking not to compromise the whole department if the worst came to the worst. It seemed to me, Ghote, that you were the man for the job.'

The Deputy Commissioner was looking at him full in the face. The liquid, all-seeing eyes saw all.

'Ghote, the case is yours and yours alone. Pursue it, man. Pursue it wherever it leads you. But pursue it yourself.'

Chapter 18

Inspector Ghote left the Deputy Commissioner's office like someone staggering in the midst of a violent rainstorm. He was hardly able to think.

He stopped in the cool dimness of the winding stone staircase leading down to the entrance of the building and stood looking sightlessly out of the narrow window slit in front of him at the quiet activity of the sun-bright compound outside. Floppy-uniformed constables were making their way here and there, wives were standing chattering to each other, children were playing in the dusty gravel. It was a placid scene. And inside his head there was turmoil. Whenever he tried to think about any one of the facts that he had just learnt it seemed as if two others, as force-driven, as oppressing, would come battering down at him. He felt himself tottering helplessly, unable even to fight his way to any sort of shelter.

Yes, it was confirmed now that Ravi Kumar was indeed the murderer of Dhartiraj. Yes, the Deputy Commissioner had feared as much all along. Yes, above all, his own investigation had by no stretch of the imagination been the star-shining ascent he had seen it as. No, he had not been selected as the man best capable of bringing to a successful conclusion the biggest case the department had had to face for years: he had been picked out as the one officer the department could afford to lose.

And there was no way out of his situation.

Like rain-filled gusts of tormented air his thoughts continued to batter this way and that.

No way out. He had been told that it was his duty to pursue the case to its logical conclusion. And that must mean the arrest and indictment of Ravi Kumar. The indictment of a god. Those court scenes he had seen so delightfully in his mind's eye, the spotlight full on the chief prosecution witness, Inspector G. V. Ghote: they would take place right enough. But the spotlight would be illuminating a figure to be reviled. The No. 1 Villain of all time. The man the whole nation would rejoice in hating, for whose downfall a million eyes would eagerly watch.

A star ascending. No. No, what he had been chosen as was to be the Fall Guy. That was what they called it. The Fall Guy.

The goat tethered to the jungle tree for the tiger to smell out, for a whole nation of clawing tigers to smell out. While up above, in the *machaan*, the sportsmen looked down.

Yet what else could they do? He could see their dilemma. That was the worst of it. He could see that for the sake of the Department someone had to be sacrificed.

But no, that was not the worst of it. Everything was the worst of it. That Ravi Kumar was a murderer, that Ganesh Vinayak Ghote was the Officer Investigating, that he had been chosen not for his as yet unrevealed abilities but for his defects, that his investigation had been successful in spite of those defects, everything.

Oh, and God, now it was clear why such a powerful figure as Seth Chagan Lal had taken such a close interest in the inquiry. Jagdish Rana must have hinted to him as well that the murder had been committed by the one impossible person. The Seth had wanted to make sure this little police inspector was keeping well away from the truth.

Well, at least he had got at the truth. At least he had done that.

He placed his hands on the rim of the big flowerpot that stood just under the window slit in front of him and gripped it.

Yes, he had at least succeeded.

Though the price of success was abject failure.

He stayed clutching the big pot as if it was some great stone that he had to lift up and fling down on to besiegers below in

156

long ago Mahratta times, as if all depended on him to save the fort from sacking, looting, rape.

Down in the compound an open police truck came to a halt under the shade of the big tamarind tree opposite and half-a-dozen armed police jumped down with their rifles and set off in a motley group in the direction of the armoury. A chicken went dust-scuffling along beside them. In the sunlight the shadows were dense and still.

And he found that, underneath all the chaos that had whirled stormlike through him, one resolution had revealed itself.

He had been put in a position from which there was no drawing back. Very well, then, he would not draw back.

Pursue, the Deputy Commissioner had said. Then pursue he would. If Ravi Kumar was the murderer of Dhartiraj, then he would arrest him under Indian Penal Code Section 201 in the proper form. He would arrest him, do what he would to stop him. And then he would strive to his utmost to see that, when the case came to the courts, it was as good a case as could be made.

Quite probably he would never get a conviction. The whole might of the best legal representation that could be secured, and the dirtiest, would be arrayed against him. Public opinion would loom like a yellowy electricity-charged sky waiting to break into thunder and lightning against him. But do what they all would, he would go on with it. He would put in front of the court, and the world – it was his duty – the very best case possible. And somewhere the truth of it would be recognized.

It was in his own office, under the familiar groan-creak-groan of his own fan, at his own desk with its familiar little defects, that he began the fight.

The first thing was to secure another interview with the suspect, and one at which he would not be able to refuse to answer questions.

But here at least life had become easier for him. If he was going, before long, to arrest Ravi Kumar – and he was – then no longer did he need to conceal his intentions at all costs.

He picked up the telephone and dialled.

'*Film Femme*, your favourite film magazine, good afternoon.'

'Miss Officewalla, please.'

She was there.

'Miss Officewalla, it is Inspector Ghote. There is yet one more thing that you can do to help me.'

'Inspector, I am very busy – '

He cut urgently across the languid and haughty voice.

'Miss Officewalla, I am wanting to put questions concerning the death of Dhartiraj to Mr Ravi Kumar.'

There. It was done. Nothing now could stop the whole worshipping nation from knowing soon that this obscure CID wallah was accusing the greatest superstar of them all of a most dastardly crime. Well, all right, let them know. Let them do what they would.

At the far end of the line there was a holy silence. It was broken at last.

'Inspector? Inspector Ghote, is it that you are still a member of the CID?'

'Please ring on another line and make fullest inquiries.'

Another silence. But a shorter one.

'Well, Inspector, I will not conceal from you that I will be doing that before I set a single finger to my typewriter. But in the meanwhile may I ask some questions?'

He drew in a breath.

'Miss Officewalla, in due course I would answer each and every one of your questions. But, madam, first there is what you can do for me. And perhaps also what I can do for you.'

'Well, Inspector, what is it? What is it?'

The vibrant eagerness contrasted sharply with the *I am very busy* of a minute or so ago.

'Miss Officewalla, you would not be altogether surprised, I think, to hear that when earlier today I attempted to put questions to Mr Kumar he refused to pay attention whatsoever.'

There came a dry chuckle down the line.

'So this is my problem, madam. I am wanting to meet him where I can speak with him without his preventing. Some sort of a public place, if you please. And, madam, I would be very happy for you to be a witness of what occurs. The sole and solitary witness, if you are liking.'

He heard the indrawn breath. The gulp and grab of the big fish taking the bait.

'Inspector, I will fix it, even if it has to be bang in the middle of the Filmfare Awards themselves.'

'The Filmfare Awards?' Here at least was some part of the *filmi* world he knew something about. The huge annual prize-giving ceremony called for traffic arrangements of such elaboration that even Crime Branch had to take cognizance of them. 'Yes, when are they taking place then?'

Miss Officewalla's hiss of dismay came clearly over the crackle and buzzing of the line.

'Inspector, they are next Sunday only. Everyone knows that.'

'Sunday. Of course, Sunday. I had not realized it would be Sunday so soon. And, of course, if that is the best occasion to confront – '

'No.'

'No, madam?'

'No, there is a better occasion. I have just seen on my desk diary here. Inspector, I take it you can wait till at least the day after tomorrow?'

'Yes,' Ghote said, 'I can afford to wait.'

'Very well then. The day after tomorrow at eleven-thirteen a.m. exactly, the time fixed by the astrologers, the *mahurat* takes place for Parvati Films International's new mythological. It is going to be a very big affair. They are paying the priests who will conduct the ceremony more than has ever been given before. None other than Baby Pinkie – the little short-pants horror – will be turning the camera. And who will have the honour of acting as Clapper Boy but Ravi Kumar himself?'

'Yes,' said Ghote. 'That would do very well.'

In the time that led up to the *mahurat* ceremony officially starting Parvati Films International's new mythological Ghote hardly ate or slept. He could think of nothing but that grim moment ahead when, with Miss Officewalla representing the eyes of all the world on him, he would have to pin down Superstar Ravi Kumar and would almost certainly end by arresting him on a charge of having murdered Dhartiraj. Though he went through the pleasures of a day off-duty as if it had been any other, the customary comforts of his home life hardly existed for him. It was not now that he despised them, as he had done when he had not been able to endure the thought of going home when he had believed he was the chosen star detective of the whole Bombay force and was heroically on the track of the greatest murderer of all time. It was simply that the task ahead, to which he was inescapably duty-bound, was so awe-inspiring, now that he had to tackle it as one simple unsupported investigating officer.

His Protima, of course, pressed him in a wifely way to take food and he had to rouse himself enough to invent a stomach upset, bad but not so bad that she would go hurrying off to borrow the neighbours' thermometer. He submitted, however, to the concoction she always made at such times and endured its mouth-wrinkling bitterness with his thoughts concentrated on the hour of 11.13 a.m. next day.

He arrived for the ceremony ridiculously early, holding in front of him the *mahurat* card which Miss Officewalla had persuaded Parvati Films to send him by messenger, a splendid piece of stationery with a folded outer cover of crisply crinkled deep red secured with a little golden tassel and inside an ornately printed thick sheet of purest white giving not only the time and the place but heart-arousing descriptions of the stars of the new film, its producer, its director, its song-writers and even of its story-writer.

For almost an hour he wandered round the studio where the ceremonial filming of a key scene from the new film was to take place, already gnawed at by anxiety in case Ravi Kumar for some reason failed to appear to perform his honorary function of acting as Clapper Boy or in case, when he did, that he would somehow still succeed in avoiding being questioned. He watched setting coolies labouring over the final erection of the set, a lavish temple with gigantic pillars and a huge flight of steps mounting up to an enormous statue of the goddess Kali – it all seemed to have been left appallingly late – and he experienced a jab of real disillusionment when that figure of weight and majesty was revealed as feather-light plastic when a carpenter toppled it with an accidental poke of his sawing elbow. Nor was it any compensation when the assistant director insisted on the lights in the goddess's jewel eyes being tested after the accident and he was able to see them glow a magnificent red.

But gradually the studio took on the look proper to the occasion. Scores of folding chairs were hastily set out. The garlands for the camera and the sound booms were hurried in, bringing with them a cool fragrance of frangipani amid the hot dust smell. Then the priests, saffron-robed, bespectacled and seemingly far distant from their surroundings, were shown up on to the marigold-hung platform built for them and the music began, the light and insistent rhythm of the drum and the throaty piping of a *shenai*. Soon the priests were chanting too.

The studio was beginning to look reasonably full at last, though none of the people arriving in a steady stream appeared to be the VIPs he was looking out for as heralds of the arrival of Ravi Kumar. A Parvati Films executive was, however, going round to various actors in costume and to the technicians handing over, with much attempt at being discreet, wads of notes from an enormously bulging wallet.

The black money payments, he thought, feeling very much an old hand at *filmi* ways now. Twenty per cent of the paper sum as extra non-accountable payments. But, of course, a much larger proportion for the stars. And what was that story Miss Officewalla had told? About the producer who was unwilling to pay up when the moment came and covered his whole head with bandages and pretended to have been in an accident so that he could not talk to the star who came to demand his money? Something like that. It seemed right for this world he had got himself into. But the killing of Dhartiraj, that had not been a matter of easy-come easy-go. That had been real. And Ravi Kumar would find out just how real before many minutes had gone by.

He looked over at the big clock that had been hung on one of the walls so that everyone could see when the auspicious moment for the starting of the film had come. Nearly eleven o'clock. Surely when that first shot, even if it was not, as Miss Officewalla had explained, the first scene, was due in only fourteen minutes' time Ravi Kumar and the other notables had left their arrival rather late. This was worse than when he had waited for Jagdish Rana to arrive at the party at the Taj.

But those people coming in now, they were stars, surely. Yes, that was Billy Banker, grinning like a monkey. And there was the Minister who, Miss Officewalla had said, was to switch on the camera. And there was that dancer – what was her name? Everybody knew it – the one who had notched up no fewer than six hundred films and was still to be seen in every cabaret or night-club scene. Well, if she had come, Ravi Kumar should not be long coming too. After all, he was, so to speak, here on duty. And, look, that must be the other star with a duty to perform, Baby Pinkie, in those pink satin shorts.

Ah, there at least was Miss Officewalla, with her beaky nose scenting and seeking this way and that. And there was another face he knew, young Kishore Sachdev. Come to see if he could get a word with the great Ravi Kumar, of course. Well, he would miss his chance. A more important matter had to be brought to the attention of Mr Kumar than any film role.

And there was Director Ghosh, come to wish his colleague at Parvati Films good luck, but not too much. And there was Seth Chagan Lal, looking richer than ever. Were those diamond buttons on that white sharkskin coat of his? Perhaps, when not only the Villian of his *Khoon Ka Gaddi* but its Hero also was swept off the scene, he would have to retrench a little.

Suddenly, from up in the high roof of the studio, a whole battery of lights plunged their hard beams down on to the set. They would be beginning at any minute. But where was the Clapper Boy?

He looked at the big clock.

Ten past eleven. The long minute hand juddered to the time just as he looked.

Where was Ravi Kumar?

In a sudden sweat-drenched panic he pushed his way through the crowd – already one or two people were standing up on their chairs – to the place where he had seen the gossip queen. Careless of the fact that she was in full flow of a joking conversation with the joshing Billy Banker, he went up to her and broke in.

'Madam. Miss Officewalla. Where is he?'

She was not put out. With a quieting gesture of her thin long-fingered hand, she gave him a rapid aside.

'He will come. Do not worry. A great star is always late.'

She turned back to the grinning comedian.

'A fan,' Ghote heard her explain briefly, as he retreated.

They were rehearsing the two stars up on the set now for the scene to be filmed. Another of the assistant directors was crouching in front of them on the huge temple steps under the stern gaze of the illuminated Kali reading over and over the lines they would have to say. *What you have done will bring dishonour to us all. It was for you that I did it.* Here the female star practised her reaching-forward gesture that conveyed how much she loved him. And he practised his stern rejection face. *For this I will cut your nose.*

They went over the little scene time and again. Miss Officewalla had said it was a key part of the story. Neither of the stars' Hindi was very well pronounced.

But suddenly there was a commotion over by the entrance doors. He swung round. His eyes took in the big clock as he did so. 11.12. Surely there would hardly be time now even if – But it was not Ravi Kumar. It was Nilima.

He turned away. It no longer mattered whether Nilima saw him make the arrest or not. It would not be the first big step up into that different world of hers. It would only be a matter of duty, with universal execration following it.

His eyes flicked back to the clock. Still 11.12. But that long minute hand must be going to judder on to the auspicious moment at any instant. The chanting of the brahmins had risen to a holy clamour.

And still no Ravi Kumar.

Baby Pinkie had been standing up on a chair by the camera for some minutes, the Cameraman at his side demonstrating just what he had to do to turn it. The Minister who was going to switch the camera on had been there for even longer, standing on the other side, Ministerial finger on the switch, a slightly be-wildered-looking figure in his plain white jacket and white Gandhi cap.

He looked at the clock again. How truly terrible if the moment was missed. How like Ravi Kumar to bring about such a disaster.

But the long minute hand still pointed firmly to 11.12.

And there, as he gazed and gazed, it firmly stayed. The *filmi* world knew how to cope with the inexorable progress of the heavenly bodies. Clocks could be fixed. Time could be made to stand still.

It must have been only five minutes after the appointed hour that Ravi Kumar arrived to perform his allotted function. And he performed it very well. Bar the fact that it was not actually taking place at the correct moment, it went without a hitch.

'Ready for Take,' an Assistant Director called out.

'Sound start,' the Director boomed through the megaphone.

Two sharp whistle blasts came from the sound booth, the exact replica of the one in which Ghote had heard the solid facts of the murder from old Ailoo. How long ago it seemed, that talk, when he had come to learn of the old coolie's unde-viating devotion to the exact limits of his task, of the younger Lights Boy who had been so badly injured when the Baby had slipped from his hand and nearly fallen on to Sudhaker Wani and all the details of what must have happened when the Five-K had been slashed from its place.

Or when Ravi Kumar, as it had now turned out, had slashed the Five-K down.

And there he was now, looking so debonair and carefree, stepping forward at the Director's shout of 'Camera' and 'Clap', holding the clapper-board unnaturally high so that everybody could see, as well as the lens of the camera, the film's title neatly written on it and in large letters the word *Mahurat*.

'*Mahurat* shot,' he called out, his voice confident and easy. 'Good luck to Parvoti Films International. Fresh laurels, fame and glory to our stars.'

And CLAP.

It was done. Hero and Heroine spoke their lines and got them right. 'Cut,' bellowed the Director in high good humour.

Clapping broke out everywhere and there were shouts of 'Shabash' 'Good luck' and 'Jolly well done.' Bearers swooped down with huge trays of snacks and drinks, and discreet words to the more important guests to indicate which glasses of fruit juice held the gin that the visiting Minister ought not to know about.

Ghote moved with purpose through the crowd. He saw that he would not need to signal to Miss Officewalla. She was approaching the smiling, laughing Ravi Kumar as steadily and swiftly as himself.

He felt a swift stab of hunter's joy at the way he eventually contrived the moment of confrontation. He succeeded in keeping himself screened from the superstar by the busily eating and drinking guests until the very last moment. He must have risen up beside him like an avenging spirit.

And for a moment – for just one moment – the handsome, confident face showed a tiny spasm of fear. It went as quickly as it had come and the cutting profile was calmly turned away, as if by looking elsewhere his own whole existence could be blotted out. But the telltale look had been there. And it gave him renewed heart.

'Mr Kumar,' he said, thrusting himself forward until his face was within three or four inches of that much photographed profile. 'Mr Kumar, am I to speak in front of all?'

The superstar turned at the words. Not quite so impossible to touch him then.

'Mr Kumar, I have enlisted the aid of Miss Officewalla here. No doubt she is well known to you. She has agreed to act as if you were giving her interview so that we can go somewhere quiet together.'

The superstar plainly took in what he had said. He clearly was working hard to make up his mind what to do.

A sense of slowly growing achievement was there to feel inside himself, like a seed little by little bursting its hard shell and forcing its way to the light. He was going to beat this man. Heavy as the dense weight of the earth his power might be, immeasurably heavier, so it might seem, than the tiny seed underneath. But that seed had its force. And it would push through.

'Well, Mr Kumar? Is it?'

'Very good.'

The fellow still kept his debonair look. But no dramatic breakdown was to be expected. The thing was that he himself was the one with the initiative now.

Miss Officewalla asked, loudly for all to hear, if Raviji would give her a short interview and, with smiling apologies to the adulating circle round him, the superstar left in her wake.

Ghote brought up the rear, knowing he would be unnoticed.

Not for the first time he thought of Miss Officewalla with gratitude. She had known at once where in all the confusion she could find somewhere to go and talk undisturbed. It was the Publicity Manager's cabin here, small and stuffy, its walls covered with posters of past triumphs, and exactly what was needed.

He positioned one of the chairs on the near side of the desk for Miss Officewalla, indicated to Ravi Kumar that he could take the Publicity Manager's own seat and made no attempt to sit down himself.

'Mr Kumar,' he began without preliminaries, 'I have evidence that approximately ten minutes before the murder of Mr Dhartiraj you were seen entering the compound of Talkiestan Studios by climbing over the back wall thereof. Is there any comment you wish to make on that?'

He kept his eyes fixed on the superstar's arrogantly handsome face as if his very life depended on his never once blinking. But he was aware that, at his side, Miss Officewalla had drawn in a quick breath as if to say 'Good God, is it that strong against him?'

He waited for his answer.

'What evidence, Inspector?' The superstar sounded totally cool. 'I am telling you it would have to be pretty remarkable to contradict the known facts.'

And his smile, the smile that had time and again enraptured a million female hearts, flashed out like a scimitar.

'I am not at liberty to reveal the names of witnesses at the present time,' he said stolidly.

At his side he felt Miss Officewalla's faith begin abruptly to seep away like water from a cracked *chhatti*.

'But,' he added, without too closely considering what he was saying, 'I can assure you, Mr Kumar, it is the evidence of a man who knows you well and it is altogether circumstantial.'

'Of a man?' the superstar asked sharply.

'Yes,' he shot back, a hot sweep of triumph running through him. 'Of a man, Mr Kumar. Not of a poor old woman rag-picker who saw what she should not and was paid for that by being carried off to God knows where.'

'What rag-picker, Inspector? Really, you seem to be talking sheer madness.'

It was coolly said. Said with diabolic coolness. A coolness that contrasted all too clearly with his own flush of raucous heat.

He swallowed hard and tried to regain his previous dominance.

'Mr Kumar, all that is neither here nor there.' But the words did not somehow sound as authoritative as they ought to have done. 'Mr Kumar, I have asked what you were doing at the time.'

'At the time poor Dhartiraj was killed, my dear fellow?'

'Yes, sir. At that time.'

He should not have said 'sir'. Damn it, he should not.

'As it happens, Inspector, I can give you an answer to your question. I have only just this moment realized it. We are at a *mahurat* now. I was at a *mahurat* then.'

'At a *mahurat*?'

He had sounded damnably confident.

'Miss Officewalla can confirm even,' the superstar said, with enormous laziness. 'She was there also. And about two hundred other people.'

'Why, yes,' Miss Officewalla said, 'Yes.'

She stood up with disconcerting suddenness and turned towards the door.

'Yes,' she said. 'I had quite forgotten that *mahurat*, Raviji.'

Chapter 19

Raviji. The term of familiarity struck Ghote like a cold knife. Miss Officewalla had lost faith in him. Ravi Kumar had with a few careless words slashed his whole case into ribbons.

But he could not have done. It was impossible. Bitter though Jagdish Rana was, he had not been lying in his description of the superstar climbing the back wall at Talkiestan Studios. He had seen him do that. And so had the old rag-picker. Or why else had she been made off with?

His mind whirred round like a slipping gearwheel. And then clicked home.

'Mr Kumar,' he said, 'at what time exactly were you at that *mahurat* where Miss Officewalla saw you?'

'That would be easy to check,' the superstar answered, as cool as ever. 'The time for every such ceremony is invariably well-known.'

'And,' said Ghote, swinging round to address not Ravi Kumar but Miss Officewalla, her long thin fingers already on the handle of the door, 'certain great stars consider it is their right always to be late, isn't it? Isn't it, Miss Officewalla?'

She let the door handle go and turned to look at the superstar with eyes already hardening against him once more.

'Yes,' she said. 'Of course he was late. How foolish of me not to think.'

Ghote turned back to Ravi Kumar.

'I am suggesting,' he said, 'that you left the Talkiestan Studios by the same way that you had entered. That you dropped in the borrowed car you were using the old long-tailed shirt you had been wearing over whatever smart clothes you had on and that you took a taxi to the *mahurat* so as not to be seen coming in an old, old car which might make people talk.'

'Yes,' Miss Officewalla broke in, her voice showing her mounting excitement. 'It was by taxi that he came. Someone sent us a photo of him arriving, and I remember thinking it was unusual for Ravi Kumar to take a taxi.'

'Well, Mr Kumar?' Ghote said.

He had not expected the superstar to break at the beginning, but he thought it was well possible that he would now.

And it seemed that he was going to.

He lifted his head in a quick challenging look.

'Yes,' he said, 'I did go into the compound at Talkiestan over the back wall.'

The slow beating of triumphal music began to sound in Ghote's head. To bring the great Ravi Kumar to court in the face of a million adoring fans would be terrible. But at least he would be doing so now with an admission in his pocket, however easily that might be withdrawn in the witness-box. Yet it was something that he had not really dared to count on achieving. And now he had it.

'Yes,' the superstar repeated, 'I entered that place like a thief in the night.'

He rose from his chair behind the Publicity Manager's untidy desk.

'But I did not go there to kill Dhartiraj,' he said. 'I admit even that I had reason enough to hate him. But I did not kill him, and I will refuse altogether to say why I entered those Studios.'

So this is the line he is going to take, Ghote thought at once. Clever enough. To admit to what there was ample evidence against him for, but to deny absolutely anything that must still be supposition. It was really the superstar way. This arrogant claim to be above questioning. This calm assumption that he could not be brought to trial like a common murderer.

Well, let him see what it felt like to be arrested. To be kept in a cell and to know that all the time everything about you was being investigated. Perhaps that would break the superstar shell and show the man beneath.

But would it?

An uneasy suspicion grew in him that it would not. There would be lawyers demanding the release of such an obviously innocent man. There would be messages going in and out of that cell, whatever precautions were taken, when it was Ravi Kumar, with all his wealth and with all the admiration that existed for him, who was needing information.

He scrabbled for some way of countering it all. Briefly despaired. Renewed his determination. And found a possibility. A daring, almost ridiculous possibility, but a possibility.

'Mr Kumar,' he said, 'I require you to accompany me straightaway to Talkiestan Studios where we will go through together all your alleged actions on the morning of Dhartiraj's murder.'

The superstar had, at once and without the least protest, agreed to the proposal. It was, Ghote realized after a little, the course that must have seemed to him to be in his own best interests. He must still hope to come out of it all, not just unharmed, but to advantage. He would have shown himself willing to indulge the police in whatever they wanted and he would have given away nothing. He would see himself as playing in the real world the role of Hero unjustly suspected but bound to be triumphantly vindicated in the last reel.

Well, they would see. Under real pressure, as intense this way as it could be made to be, he might crack.

Words from the great Hans Gross's mildew-marked volume, long ago committed to memory, came back to him. They were from the pages headed 'When the Witness Does Not Wish to Speak the Truth' and they seemed to fling a bridge for him all at once to the days of simplicity before the notion had got into his head that he had been somehow chosen to be a star detective. 'The Investigator is the calmer of the two. For the Witness is playing a dangerous game while the worst that can happen to the Investigator is once more to be made a fool of.' If only he could hold on to that, then perhaps, even with all the superconfidence of the superstar, Ravi Kumar would yet betray himself.

So they went, superstar, investigator and, representing in her beak-nosed person all watching India, Miss Officewalla, once more to the Talkiestan Studios. And, such was the influence even without a word being said of the great Ravi Kumar, that shooting was halted on Sound Stage No. 2 and the set for Maqbet's throne-room was hastily re-installed while up above on the plank-wide catwalk a new Five-K was fitted at the exact spot where the one that had fallen to kill Dhartiraj had been. Even the curve-bladed dagger that had been used to slash those ropes was brought by Assistant Inspector Jahdev from its safe-keeping. A small-part actor was found to take the murdered star's part, eagerly volunteered indeed, and the red robes Dhartiraj had been wearing were brought out again for him to wear.

Swaying-bellied Director Ghosh, Cameraman – no, Director of Photography – Chandubhai, his assistants, the Sound Recordist, old Ailoo were all summoned to take their former places. Even Nilima, at work elsewhere in the Studios, hearing of what was going on, presented herself ready to play her part. And Ghote, with the new realism that had come to him ever since he had learnt that he was no star but more a convenient extra, thought to himself that no doubt she was determined to steal the scene if the least opportunity arose.

At last all was ready. Ghote turned to the superstar.

'Very well, Mr Kumar,' he said, his voice as grimly matter-of-fact as he could make it. 'We will go to the start now and proceed.'

Ravi Kumar turned without a word and followed him. The car was waiting just outside the narrow door of the studio. They climbed in, himself, his witness and the necessary Miss Officewalla. In three minutes they were in the long street at the back of the compound. Ghote told the driver to park just inside the lane on the far side from the blue-painted temple. They got out and stood in a little awkward group under the slow stares of the proprietors and customers of the little dark shops at the lane entrance.

'It was here that you waited in that borrowed car?' Ghote asked the superstar, though he hardly made the words into a question.

Ravi Kumar gave him a suddenly sharp look.

'Yes, it was,' he said, sounding just a little put out.

'Very well,' Ghote said brusquely, 'we will assume that whatever time you waited till you thought the lane opposite was all clear has gone by. Please proceed accordingly.'

Without any comment Ravi Kumar set out across the street,

dodged just behind a slow bullock-drawn big-barrelled water-cart, its dangling jug clank-clanking as it went, and headed for the narrow entrance between the temple and the Moon Winding Works.

The cigarette-vendor, perched up on a thin stone shelf under his stall, watched them go by, coughing hard, his eyes darting with curiosity.

Ravi Kumar strode down the lane ahead of them, setting a pace that seemed to reflect a certain nervous tension. Ghote saw that he gave just one quick glance to a heap of paper scraps, doubtless the place where the old rag-picker Kesar had been lying unnoticed by him as he first went down towards the banyan.

Good, he thought. Keep up the pressure.

They reached the tree.

'Go in under,' Ghote said, pressing hard.

Ravi Kumar stepped under the rope-hung shade of the old tree.

'Go up. Just as you did before.'

Without a word, the superstar seized one of the dangling roots and hauled himself upwards. In a few seconds he was on top of the high wall. The coiled-back strands of the barbed wire he had cut before vibrated a little as he arrived.

Ghote turned to Miss Officewalla.

'Madam, would you care to go back round in my vehicle?' he asked. 'I am intending to accompany Mr Kumar all the way.'

'Yes, very good, Inspector.'

She sounded subdued, more so than he had ever heard her. He welcomed it. It was a sign that the intangible pressure he was trying to build up really existed.

He turned, stepped under the banyan, caught hold of the same dangling root that Ravi Kumar had done – fibrous and harsh to the touch – and swung himself up as easily on to the broad top of the wall.

'Now, he said, 'how long exactly did it take to cut these wires?'

'I don't – About two minutes. Two minutes, or less.'

He pushed his shirt-cuff clear of his watch.

'Then we will wait,' he said.

He stood beside the superstar in silence. Down in front of them in the Studios compound they could see the tree underneath which Jagdish Rana parked his unimpressive car. A dog went ambling along in the sunshine and smelt at it. Around them was the old sharp odour of bird droppings.

He allowed three full minutes to go by on his watch, and then another half. He saw that there was a sheen of sweat on the superstar's forehead although they were well shaded from the sun.

'Very well. Show me the way you got down.'

But it was not difficult to see how it would have been done. The keys of that gigantic, pink-painted typewriter, peeling here and there now, led down like so many rock steps to the ground below. Ravi Kumar jumped down them with every appearance of casual ease.

But he put a foot wrong on the lowest one and for a moment had difficulty keeping his balance.

Close behind, Ghote leapt right over the last two of the keys to land with a neat thump just at the superstar's back.

'So, he said, 'you then went quickly up to the end of this passage and at the top you looked this way and that. Then, since there was nobody about – or nobody that you could see – you went quickly along to the door of the Sound Stage No. 2. Please carry out the same procedure again.'

Ravi Kumar turned his head, as if to make sure that any sign of stress that might show on his face would not be observed. But he set off at once.

At his heels Ghote saw, when they came to the head of the passage between the Property Department and the side of Sound Stage No. 2, that Miss Officewalla was already there. She watched the superstar hurry along to the narrow door into the studios with the eyes on either side of her beak of a nose positively glinting.

'You went in,' he said sharply when the superstar hesitated for a moment at the door.

They all three entered. Inside it was as black as he remembered from his first visit coming to investigate the circumstances of Dhartiraj's death within an hour of its occurrence.

'Please do as exactly as possible what you did before,' he said to the superstar.

'Certainly.'

Was there a little relaxation, now that he guessed that his actions on the previous occasion had not been observed beyond this point? The pressure must be screwed up again.

He followed the superstar's pale silk shirt through the darkness. He was led directly towards the corner, not far away, from which the ladder led up in the dark to the catwalk where the Five-K hung. The route took them quite close to the table with the curve-bladed dagger on it. 'Is this a dagger that I see before me?' Yes. He could just spot it there. It would be the work of a second only to dart aside and seize it.

But Ravi Kumar did not so much as glance at the faintly glinting shape on the table. Instead he went straight to the foot of the narrow iron ladder.

'Mr Kumar,' he said sharply, 'have you followed exactly the path you took before?'

He had wondered briefly whether to accuse him directly of having avoided going to the table with the dagger. But he felt it vital at this stage not to risk pretending to more knowledge than he had. If the superstar had, for instance, come this far and then gone back for the dagger, to have claimed to have known otherwise could well let go like steam from a suddenly pierced vessel the pressure he hoped he was keeping up.

'Well? Have you?' he jabbed out, in face of the superstar's silence.

'Oh yes, Inspector. I have.'

Was there a tiny note of mockery there? It must not be.

'But you did not just stand here,' he snapped out. 'Please go on and do just what you did before.'

The superstar turned to the ladder in silence. He began to climb up. He seemed not to be going as fast as he might have done.

Ah, the nerves strained again.

And then the pale blue splodge of colour up in the darkness ahead ceased to move.

'Well, go on, go on. You did not just go three-quarters of the way up that ladder and then stop. Go on, Mr Kumar.'

'But, Inspector, that is just what I did do.'

The voice coming down from the darkness was openly mutinous.

He glanced upwards.

That attitude must be crushed. Crushed at once. Or he would lose him altogether.

'So this is to be your story, is it?' he said to the dimly-seen figure. 'Very well then. If you say that you stopped where you are, from now on I require you to do what I say.'

He wheeled round, darted over to the table where the dagger was, seized it, was back at the ladder's foot in two bounds and up half a dozen rungs as quickly.

He thrust the dagger upwards, handle foremost.

'Here,' he said. 'Here. Take. Take this and do exactly what I direct you to do.'

'Certainly, Inspector.'

He was losing him. Damn it, he was losing him. But why? Nothing for it but to press him and press him still.

'Go on up,' he ordered.

He turned rapidly to Miss Officewalla.

'Madam, I am going up too. But I do not think a catwalk is a suitable place for a lady. Please wait here and watch closely from below.'

'Very well, Inspector.'

At least she was still subdued.

He started up the ladder behind the superstar and the moment he had reached the top he directed him sharply to cross the catwalks to the place where the new Five-K hung. The superstar seemed to take the creaking and the slight sway of the planks beneath their feet very much for granted. Was this just that the man who had bounded down so easily from that ornate saddle on top of the sports car when they had been shooting that village scene was naturally well-balanced? Or was it that the rocking groaning path they were taking was one already familiar to him? Surely he had made this journey holding that dagger in this way before.

They reached their destination.

The superstar stood directly above the new Five-K.

'Well, Inspector,' he said, his voice distinctly mocking now, 'am I to cut the ropes? It won't do that chap below much good, but if you insist.'

Thinking hard how to snatch back the lost initiative, Ghote stood looking down at the brightly-lit figure on the red *gaddi* below. Damn it, how was he to regain the grip he had had not so long ago? And he must. He must.

And abruptly he knew what might do it.

He looked up and faced the superstar boldly.

'Yes,' he said. 'Yes, Mr Kumar. Do just that. Stoop down to use the knife on those ropes. Do everything but actually cut them. Go on. Kneel and use the blade. Now. Do it now.'

It was what the fellow had surely done just those few days ago. Make him do it again then. Test him. Test him to the very limit. And see if he would break.

Very slowly, without another word being said, Ravi Kumar turned and knelt on both knees on the narrow catwalk. Below him it was just possible to make out the ropes holding the dangling Five-K. The blade of his curved dagger caught the light as he moved it towards them.

And then it stopped.

In the darkness Ravi Kumar swiftly straightened up. He swung round. The knife blade was glinting in front of him.

'No, Inspector,' he said in a voice little above a whisper. 'I will not do it.'

Had he got him now? Had he?

The glinting blade moved suddenly, lunging nearer.

In a single instant his mouth went parchedly dry. He found himself swaying urgently backwards on the narrow plank beneath his feet.

And stopped himself.

He must not show fright. He must act as if fear was an impossibility.

'You will not do it, Mr Kumar?' he asked.

His voice sounded extraordinarily level. He marvelled at it.

'No, Inspector,' the superstar's voice came back in the darkness.

It seemed more tremor-filled by far than his own.

'No, Inspector, it turns out that I would rather tell you the truth.'

So this was the moment. He had done it after all.

'Go on,' he said, hardly breathing the words.

'Inspector, I did not know I was so weak-stomached. But to go through doing what that fellow must have done. It's ridiculous. But I cannot.'

'That fellow'. The implication was clear: some other person. But had he not pushed him up to the edge and over?

'Go on, Mr Kumar,' he said, quietly again.

'Inspector, it is not an easy thing to tell. But I – I was here that morning for a private reason, Inspector.'

He leant forward in the dark as near as he could get to the superstar's face. He wanted to see, if he could, its exact expression. The voice had certainly betrayed some deep inner trouble. But what exactly? Would some contraction of the features in that cuttingly handsome face betray it?

The dagger blade glinted terribly near to his unprotected stomach. But he must behave as if that simply did not exist.

Should he murmur some encouragement to go on? No, it was coming again.

'Inspector, you are a married man?'

'Of course.'

'Did you fall in love with your wife, Inspector, after you were married? In love? Really in love?'

'Yes,' Ghote said, remembering a strange, almost hallucinated time. 'Yes, I did.'

'Inspector, I am in love.'

Meena, Ghote thought. That thin, ill creature he had interviewed, the 'keep' Dhartiraj had stolen from the all-conquering superstar who had once stolen his wife from him, the *bachchi* star who was to have played Rani Maqbet in *Khoon Ka Gaddi* before Nilima took over the role. So that, after all, was his motive.

'Go on,' he said. 'Tell me. Tell me everything.'

'I love her, Inspector. Ill or well, thin or not, I love her. I tried that morning to telephone her at his house because I knew he was on the board to be shooting here. They said she was not at

177

home. I did not know if they were lying to me. I had to see her. I thought she must have come here with him. But I did not want anyone, not one single soul, to know that I, Ravi Kumar, had come down to chasing that girl wherever she was. So I took my servant's old shirt and a headcloth, and I borrowed a car from one of my *chumchas*. I drove to that place by the back wall that I had happened to notice, and I came in here. To see if she was here, Inspector. With him. And I climbed that ladder, Inspector.'

Now. Now it was finally coming.

'But, Inspector, only to where I showed you. From there you can see all the studio. And she was not here, Inspector. So I left. I left just seconds before that fellow cut the ropes over Dharti-raj. I heard the noise of it as I crept towards the door, but I did not know what it was. And that is all, Inspector. That is the truth.'

Chapter 20

To believe Ravi Kumar or not. Ghote stood in the darkness, at the very scene of the crime, feeling the roped plank beneath his feet still swaying a little from the force of the superstar's gestures as he had confessed his secret, and set out to weigh all the circumstances in equal pans.

First, was this no more than an attempt to pull the wool over his own eyes? Was Ravi Kumar, increasingly desperate at the unexpected closeness of the hunters, attempting to tell some just likely story, and one that had a good deal of feeling in it, so as to secure his sympathies? To blind him to the truth? It would be a superstar's answer: relying on that magnetism of his. Yet on the other hand it could not but have cost a man of his pride, a man up there, more than it was easy to realize to have to admit that he had been beaten by a rival in love and that he was even reduced to the meanest stratagems just to make sure that the girl was not in his company.

It was not difficult to imagine how having all this come out in

178

open court, to be printed in the papers and the *filmi* magazines, would be almost death to him. Yet had it not perhaps been risked just so as to escape precisely from a sentence of death?

But what if in fact Ravi Kumar had not killed Dhartiraj? What if he had done no more than what he had said?

Then someone else must be the murderer.

The superstar had not uttered a word since his plea. In the dark he was awaiting judgement. Standing, still and spent.

Ghote looked down again to the very spot where Dhartiraj had died. Nothing had changed there. Ravi Kumar's confession, delivered in that low intense voice, could not have penetrated to anyone on the ground. They were standing or sitting simply waiting to know if anything would emerge from this recon-struction. No doubt most of them were puzzling pleasantly about the superstar's presence. But only Miss Officewalla would have any idea that the great man had been undergoing trial. Trial by ordeal.

But what if he had not been enduring that ordeal? What if he had been only concerned to avoid a terrible embarrassment? Why, if Ravi Kumar was not the murderer of Dhartiraj, then Inspector Ghote no longer faced the prospect of appearing in court accusing India's most popular idol.

A burden, an almost intolerable burden, would have been lifted from his shoulders.

And it could be so. Ravi Kumar's story could be true. There was not a single fact that contradicted it.

He smiled wryly to himself in the gloom. Yet another suspect believed totally to be guilty and found after not so long to be innocent. First Jagdish Rana, the murderer from thwarted am-bition. Then Sudhaker Wani, seen as a threatened blackmailer striking back. Next young Kishore Sachdev, seen as reacting against brutally crushed hopes. Was Ravi Kumar just one more in that shameful parade?

No. No, he was not. His was a different case. With the others that absurd ambition so suddenly sparked up in him when he had believed himself chosen as a star investigator had led him into ridiculously seized-on judgements led on by the hope of achieving a star-like and startling success. But with Ravi Kumar it had been truly different. There he had discovered someone with a real motive for killing the victim, who had no actual alibi but who had tried with every trick he could produce to fabricate one, someone who had all but been in the very place where the killer must have stood at the moment of the crime. No, there was no shame in having tracked down Ravi Kumar.

And still there was only his word for it that he was not in fact Dhartiraj's killer.

Yet that word had carried a lot of conviction. There was something that could not be denied. And, if it was so, it would lift the burden. It had lifted it. Rightly or wrongly, at this moment he was feeling nothing but a tremendous sense of relief, a balloon lightness.

Unseeingly he looked down at the red-robed figure below of the actor playing the part of Dhartiraj.

And a totally new consideration was borne in on him. One that abruptly turned everything about the case upside-down.

If Ravi Kumar had been telling the truth, then at the time Dhartiraj's killer was supposed to be climbing that ladder to get to the catwalk the superstar himself had been three-quarters of the way up it. It was impossible as a route to the Five-K hanging like a convenient doom over Dhartiraj's head. And – the image of the hanging light brought this to him – here was a sliver of confirmation for the superstar's claim: surely the murderer must have been in the studio earlier so as to see that the Five-K threatened the figure on the *gaddi* below, and Ravi Kumar had not been there.

So it seemed very possible that the picture he had had of the crime all along, a picture shared by everybody he had talked to, was simply not so. No one had climbed that ladder. They could not have done so.

But, if that was the truth, how had the Five-K come to be cut loose? Because it had been. Nothing was more certain than that. A knife, almost certainly the curved dagger Ravi Kumar was still holding towards him, had sliced through those ropes. And that must have been done with the intention of killing Dhartiraj. He would, from this point of view, have been an absolutely

180

clear target. Looking down at that actor there now, that much was totally evident.

But how had the murderer got to the Five-K then?

The answer came to him.

Old Ailoo had told him it. At the very beginning of the inquiry. You could, he had said, swing dangerously on a rope from one catwalk to the other. And that is what the murderer must have done. He must have crept up another ladder, gone behind old Ailoo as he sat concentrated entirely on the light that was his charge, and have daringly swung across.

He looked. It would be possible, at least for a lights coolie used to these heights and the precarious holds, or for some sort of acrobat. A lights coolie? He considered the notion. Well, by some barely imaginable chain of circumstances, true, there might be a Lights Boy who might have some grudge against Dhartiraj, the all-popular, that would have made him want to kill him. But it was highly unlikely, and nothing that any of Assistant Inspector Jahdev's minute inquiries had turned up had showed the least sign that such a person existed.

But then no one, it seemed, would have wanted to kill that friendly figure, with the single exception of Ravi Kumar.

Now if it had been Sudhaker Wani sitting down there on the *gaddi* then dozens of people might have had a motive. The stand-in with his dubious activities of all sorts must have made plenty of people fear and hate him. Was it possible that the killer had thought Sudhaker Wani would be sitting on the *gaddi* and not Dhartiraj? It was. As far as anyone down on the ground was concerned since, until Dhartiraj had suddenly demanded extra jewels for his turban, it had been expected that the stand-in would take his place. But no one up on the catwalk could have mistaken the two. It was totally plain from here at this moment that it was the small-part actor sitting there now. No, if it was to turn out that someone had swung across to the Five-K wanting to kill Sudhaker Wani, then it would have to be a figure as laughable as a short-sighted acrobat.

And then he realized that the notion of a short-sighted acrobat was not laughable at all. Such a person existed, had been in the studio, had a strong motive.

He stood still on the narrow, slightly swaying plank beneath him, frozen with awe at his discovery.

Nothing seemed to have changed. Yet how much had. He was still staring downwards. Ravi Kumar was still, only seconds in fact after he had ended his admission, awaiting his verdict. What had made the idea flash in on him, showing him in an instant all the facts that he had known all along? What had tumbled the wall after high wall of prejudice that had prevented him seeing?

First of those walls, and most appalling, had been the one built up by his idea of himself as superstar investigator. It had simply deterred him again and again from using the old and well-tried ways of his craft. He had attempted, ridiculously, to hit on a super-solution instead of patiently discovering the facts, carefully testing them and eventually quietly seeing the conclusion that they led to. Next he had been blinded by the notion, shared by everybody, that the murder had been committed by someone taking the route to the spot that seemed most obvious. Well, they had not. And, once he had seen that, everything had begun to look different. And lastly, perhaps excusable but a grave error all the same, there had been the idea that the murderer had to be a man. He himself, not ten minutes ago, had even said to Miss Officewalla that a catwalk was no place for a lady.

But there were women who played with heights as a child plays with its toys. Women, indeed, who had as children played with heights. Professional acrobats, members of entertainers' families.

And there was a woman, in the studio at the time of Dhartiraj's death, who had begun life as just such an entertainer, a fact that was well known to every reader of *filmi* magazines, a fact he himself had been told by Miss Officewalla. And he had seen with his own eyes that that practised acrobat was extremely poor-sighted.

Nilima.

Nilima, the ageing Nilima, who had gained the coveted role of Rani Maqbet at the expense of the young Meena when the *bachchi* star had inexplicably lost her youthfully luscious curves.

182

Nilima, who had been photographed even handing Meena a friendly glass of sweet and sugary cane-juice. And had not Sudhaker Wani himself admitted that his old aunt made up mixtures which, while not fatal, did make people thinner as they liked to be in the West? What a hold on a rich star the money-hungry stand-in must have thought he had. And, when that Baby light had fallen some weeks before and had so nearly killed him, what ideas it must have put into Nilima's head. And then suddenly to have seen the dangling Five-K when she had already heard Director Ghosh say he wanted the stand-in to sit on the *gaddi* to be lit. It all fitted together so conclusively.

Yes, Nilima was the murderer.

And the world-heavy burden of indicting a nation-popular superstar had come on to his shoulders once more. The golden Nilima. The burden was yet heavier.

She had gone by the time he got down to the ground. He had had first to tell Ravi Kumar, however briefly, that he accepted his version of events, and that his secret would be safe with him. In the confusion of it all, he was a little worried that he had even indicated why he had changed his view of the whole affair. But, all too soon, the superstar would know in any case.

It seemed, however, when he at last got down and began asking for Nilima, that as soon as everybody had dispersed to their places for the reconstruction – and how stupid it had been, looking back, not to have properly accounted for Nilima when that dispersal had taken place at the time of the murder – the golden star had simply left the studio. She had, in fact, left the compound altogether. The chowkidars eventually reported that her Mercedes had gone through the gates, her driver at the wheel as usual.

But from there on she seemed to have disappeared. He had gone immediately to her home, only to be told that she had not arrived there. Her mother said she had had no other engagement after her shift at Talkiestan and that she had been expected to come home.

So then it had been a question of telephoning, with the advice of Miss Officewalla, every place she might have gone to. It had been a time-consuming search. And it became all the more baffling when, some two hours later, her driver was reported as having returned to the house with the Mercedes, but no Nilima. He had taken her, he said, to a big block of flats off Altamount Road where she often went to visit a former female star, now almost forgotten. But she had not come out to the car again and, when he had inquired, he was told she had never visited her friend. Miss Officewalla confirmed the likelihood of all this. The ex-star was much relied on for advice, she said. And there were also a good many different ways out of that particular block.

But she told him not to worry. Nilima had disappeared in this way before. She made almost a habit of rushing off to shrines all over India to seek spiritual guidance at what she felt were tricky points in her career. Only last year she had caused a great sensation by disappearing in much the same way as this, and it had turned out that she had gone in secret up to Jammu to learn whether she should retire or not. The answer had, of course, been 'No'.

'It must be the same time,' Miss Officewalla assured him. 'And, if you will promise me to keep a secret of greatest importance, I can tell you without fail when you will see her again.'

He promised, with all the solemnity he could muster.

Miss Officewalla considered.

'Very well then,' she said eventually, 'I will confide in you, Inspector, what I have pledged myself to tell nobody else in the whole wide world.'

'Yes?'

'Inspector, I know who is to receive "Best Actress" at the Filmfare Awards on Sunday. It is Nilima, Inspector. And, believe me, nothing that there is will prevent her being there for that.'

With this hope he had to be content.

The moment had almost come. The time when he would have to step out from the darkness at the side of the stage at the Shanmukhananda Hall, biggest in Asia, and, under the beating-down glare of all those lights, go up to Nilima, while she was

184

still clutching the statuette of Best Actress, still all radiant smiles, and arrest her on a charge of murder.

The idea came into his head of simply leaving, of pretending that he had never experienced that sudden coming-together up there high above Sound Stage No. 2 at Talkiestan Studios, of simply slipping away. But he squared his shoulders and pushed the thought firmly down.

Nilima had murdered Dhartiraj. He was the officer in charge of the inquiry. He would arrest her under Indian Police Code Section 201.

Looking out at the rows of stars and dignitaries on the stage in front of him, wilting and sweating on their upright chairs under the heat of the lights, he found himself quite unworried by the fact that Nilima had not yet come to take her place among them. A lot of other top stars were as late. Miss Officewalla, flitting here and there through the huge hall – busy gathering flavoursome titbits for her brew of gossip, had told him that she had no doubts whatever that the golden star would come to claim her award, and he was content.

He had plenty of time. They were still handing out the statuettes for the Technical Awards, best cinematography (colour), best cinematography (black-and-white), best audiography, best screenplay, best dialogue. The huge show had been going for little over an hour. It was only half past ten. And he was going to wait to play his part in it, which would be as undramatic as he could make it, but more dramatic all the same by far and by far than any of the tears of joy and the embraces that greeted each award as it came.

He was going to let Nilima receive her prize. He felt that he owed her that. It must mean so much to her when she was in the last years of her career, in its last months in all probability. There would have had to have come a time when she could no longer appear before the cameras as the most glamorous creature of all. The inexorable wrinkles could not have been held back for ever. Not by all the creams and oils. Not by whatever magical mixtures she could buy, at whatever cost, from people like Sudhaker Wani's old aunt. Not by all the electronic and hormone treatments that the ingenuity of Europe and America could provide. The time would have to have come when she would have to submit to the oblivion of being unfilmed. This was, and Miss Officewalla had confirmed it, almost certainly the last chance she would ever have had of receiving a Filmfare Award. He would let her take it, and have one short moment of joy from it.

Then he would step into that glare and do his duty.

He felt a sudden flutter in his stomach. And quelled it.

No, if it meant shrieking mobs of fans hounding him every day, if it meant that his name would be remembered longer than Nilima's as the man who had tried to pull down the airy edifice of light that was the *filmi duniya*, why then it would have to be so. No doubt he would have the very greatest difficulty in securing a conviction against her. It would be as difficult as he had imagined it was going to be over Ravi Kumar. More so, in that he could so easily be made out to be cruelly attacking a defenceless woman and India's darling. But he would bring his case. He would make his arrest. Nilima was the murderer he had been ordered to find. And that was that.

He looked out from the comforting darkness at the brightly lit platform.

But what if, in spite of Miss Officewalla, she did not come after all? What if she had somehow – though it was not possible – heard something down below there at the Talkiestan Studios when he had listened to Ravi Kumar's confession of hopeless love? What if, when he had at last told the superstar that he believed him, she had – but it was not possible – somehow gathered that he now knew that she was the person he wanted? He had almost certainly mumbled her name to Ravi Kumar in his confusion and haste. What if even now she was in America or England or Germany on the way to being beyond his reach?

The burden would be lifted. He would not have to step out there under the glare. He would not have to put himself up as a target for all the vilification and abuse that the golden star's countless defenders could find to hurl at him. It would be a release.

But no, it would be a worse fate than what he would have to do in a few minutes' time. He would then be to the public the man who had failed to avenge Dhartiraj, and to himself he would be a man who had failed to carry out his duty.

No, it was the lights for him. It had to be.

In the dark someone blundered into him. He turned. It was Ravi Kumar, Ravi Kumar coming to take the empty chair reserved for him out there.

'I am sorry, Mr Kumar,' he apologized.

The superstar looked at him. He flashed out a smile, the smile reserved for nameless fans. He turned and walked on to the stage, with that swagger that said 'I know a thousand eyes are on me'. There was a great storm of applause, thundering up to the platform like surge after surge of the sea. Ravi Kumar raised his clasped hands over his head in acknowledgement. He beamed. He breathed in the adoration. This was his element.

Briefly, watching from the dark, he recalled that, not so long ago, he had held for a few mad days, the notion that he too could live in a similar element. Could be an adulated detective. How absurd.

But now surely the moment before him could not be long away. If Ravi Kumar had come, could Nilima be far behind? The Minister who was handing out the awards – no mere State office-holder, but the Minister of Defence from Delhi himself – was picking up the statuette to go to the Best Supporting Actress and the roll of nominations was being sonorously proclaimed. Even the Hollywood star who was a guest of honour – what was he called? Those American names were all so hard to remember – was sitting up and looking more alert than he had managed to do for many minutes. It would not be very long now. No doubt Nilima had kept her entrance until after this award. She might be waiting somewhere in the darkness behind him now. But she would come.

Then, just as the name of the winner was read out and the explosion of applause followed, a figure did come sliding up behind him in the darkness. For an instant he thought it was her. Was she coming to speak to him? To appeal to him? As she had appealed once before – but that must have been mere cunning, mere making sure that this policeman was not getting anywhere near her.

But it was quite a different figure that emerged from the shadows. Miss Officewalla, tall and beaky.

'Inspector.'

'Yes? Yes? What is it? She has gone? You have heard something?'

'Yes, Inspector. I have just had a telephone call.'

'She has fled away to Europe? To America?'

'No, Inspector. She has not fled. Perhaps it is worse. Perhaps better.'

'Yes? Yes? What?'

'Inspector, you know that big circus that there is at present on the Oval Maidan by Churchgate?'

'Yes, yes.'

What was this? Circuses?

'Inspector, it seems that she went in there just half an hour ago. I do not know whether she persuaded them or what. But she climbed up to the very top of the tent. And then she threw herself to death, Inspector.'

It was a shock. But it was a shock that sent his mind racing. He seemed to know for certain everything that had happened. Yes, Nilima had gone to consult some shrine when she had left the Talkiestan Studios so suddenly. She must have wanted guidance badly. But she had come back to Bombay, just as Miss Officewalla had said she would, to collect her Award. And before setting out for the hall she must have rung up Ravi Kumar to find out if anything had happened in her absence. And he had told her what he had guessed from those mumbled words of his own up above the scene of Dhartiraj's death, that she was certain to be arrested for the murder. And so she had taken that way out. The woman who had begun as the child of a family of poor acrobats and had risen to such heights had decided to end her life in the circus, climbing high as she could and then falling, falling.

It was a fitting end. A fitting *filmi* end.

He stood thinking about her for a little longer, not formulating any ideas that could be expressed in words, simply feeling what it was that she had been and the sadness of it.

Then the thought of what this had done to his own situation

rose up. Well, the answer to the riddle of Dhartiraj's death would never now be more than a confidential entry on the files. No execration for him as the persecutor of a golden heroine. And no glory as the man who had broken the case of the murdered star. Some public blame for an apparently unsolved mystery. Some recognition for what he had done from his superiors perhaps. A quiet end to it all.

Well, perhaps it was best. Perhaps that was a fitting end to it for him too.

MORE ABOUT PENGUINS
AND PELICANS

Penguinews, which appears every month, contains
details of all new books issued by Penguins
as they are published. From time to time it is
supplemented by our stocklist, which includes around
5,000 titles.

A specimen copy of *Penguinews* will be sent to you
free on request. Please write to Dept EP, Penguin
Books Ltd, Harmondsworth, Middlesex, for your copy.

In the U.S.A.: For a complete list of books available
from Penguins in the United States write to Dept CS,
Penguin Books, 625 Madison Avenue, New York,
New York 10022.

In Canada: For a complete list of books available from
Penguins in Canada write to Penguin Books Canada Ltd,
2801 John Street, Markham, Ontario L3R 1B4.